About the Author

Rupert Ellenborough served in Northern Ireland during the Troubles. This is his first novel. He and his wife live in rural Northamptonshire surrounded by their six dogs.

Trouble

Rupert Ellenborough

Trouble

Vanguard Press

VANGUARD PAPERBACK

© Copyright 2025
Rupert Ellenborough

The right of Rupert Ellenborough to be identified as author of
this work has been asserted by him in accordance with the
Copyright, Designs and Patents Act 1988.

All Rights Reserved

No reproduction, copy or transmission of this publication
may be made without written permission.
No paragraph of this publication may be reproduced,
copied or transmitted save with the written permission of the publisher, or in
accordance with the provisions
of the Copyright Act 1956 (as amended).

Any person who commits any unauthorised act in relation to this publication
may be liable to criminal prosecution and civil claims for damages.

A CIP catalogue record for this title is available from the British Library.

ISBN 978-1-83794-456-9

This is a work of fiction. Names, characters, businesses, places, events and
incidents are either the products of the author's imagination or used in a
fictitious manner. Any resemblance to actual persons, living or dead, or actual
events is purely coincidental.

*Vanguard Press is an imprint of
Pegasus Elliot Mackenzie Publishers Ltd.*
www.pegasuspublishers.com

First Published in 2025

**Vanguard Press
Sheraton House Castle Park
Cambridge England**

Printed & Bound in Great Britain

Dedication

I dedicate this book to my lovely wife, Grania.

Chapter One
West Belfast 1976

At least it had stopped raining. Second Lieutenant Colin Smith, serving in a Guards battalion, looked up at the dismal Belfast night sky. It had rained every day since the battalion had landed at Aldergrove Airport a month earlier. Colin thought gloomily that it would probably start raining again before the end of his patrol. He shivered in the cold.

Their patrol numbered twelve in total, divided into three groups. Two groups, each of four, were on foot with another four soldiers in a Land Rover. It was Colin's job to command all three groups via a small pocket radio with an earpiece attached to his right ear. All the patrols were in combat dress and wearing flak jackets, which might block a round fired from a pistol but would provide little protection against a shot from an Armalite, the IRA's preferred weapon. Everyone carried a 7.62mm self-loading rifle attached by a sling to the wrist to prevent losing the rifle in a close-quarter fight. One member of each group carried a riot gun for firing plastic bullets, in case they were needed to face a riot. However, they had been on patrol for just over an hour with nothing to report, apart from some verbal abuse from some youths outside

Murphy's Bar. It had not escalated to stone (or half-brick) throwing, and so the riot guns had not been needed.

It was time to move onto Springfield Road and head east towards the Lower Falls. This was a difficult time for the patrol because the Provisional IRA knew they had to take this route. The dogs started barking as they made their approach. The smell of coal fires grew stronger as they moved east. Colin glanced across the road at Guardsman Pierce and could see the tension on his face. Pierce had been reduced in rank from corporal to guardsman earlier in the day for picking a fight with a paratrooper in a pub the night before the tour. The para had lost two teeth, and Pierce had lost two chevrons. Colin could see the fresh marks on his sleeve where the chevrons had just been removed.

Colin's patrol was level with Colinward Street, and they were just preparing to move when suddenly a very loud bang erupted from nearby. The patrols all took cover and made their weapons ready. Colin never ceased to wonder how a group of four soldiers could nearly vanish when taking cover in doorways and alleyways on Belfast streets. The near darkness helped, and the few working street lamps gave out only a feeble light. Colin's radio crackled noisily in his ear, and one of the patrols under his command reported a car backfiring one street away. He felt a wave of relief wash through his body, and he ordered his patrol to get up and continue their progress down Colinward Street.

As Colin and his men began to head south down Colinward Street, he turned to look behind his patrol. He wanted to check that at least one of their group members was covering their rear, remembering the warnings about being shot in the back from their Northern Ireland training. The patrol still had their rifles ready following the car backfiring minutes earlier. Colin had taken this route many times over the last month, and he had previously identified an upstairs window of a derelict house on the Clonard side of Springfield Road, which offered a full view of Colinward Street. As usual, he looked at the window through the sight of his rifle, expecting to see nothing. Instead, despite the gloom, he saw a tiny flicker of movement and, at the same time, heard a series of cracks above his head. With his rifle still ready, he released the safety catch and fired three rounds into the window. At the same time, he saw Pierce slump to the ground on the side of the street. Colin ripped open his field dressing and ran over to Pierce, whose face was already very white. Blood from a large wound in his shoulder was pumping out all over his body, transforming the patches from his discarded chevrons into a dark red stain.

The months of training before the tour kicked in, as if Colin were on automatic pilot. After trying to stem the flow of blood from Pierce's shoulder, he checked that the medics were on the way to his location. He ordered four men to guard Pierce while he and three others made a hot pursuit towards the derelict building on Springfield Road, which appeared to be the gunman's fire position. It was very difficult to enter the building from the front with the door and ground windows boarded up. Colin and his patrol rushed round to the rear of the building, where they saw an open door swinging precariously on its hinges. They burst inside, paying no attention to the threat of booby traps or improvised explosive devices, and quickly cleared the empty building. If the gunman had ever been in the building, it was impossible to tell in the almost pitch-black darkness.

If Colin had expected any sympathy from his company commander after the shooting incident, he soon realised that this was in very short supply. After a cursory examination by the company medic to check that he was not seriously injured, he was told to write a full account of the incident and report it to the company commander as soon as possible.

Major Jeremy Kershaw did not particularly like Colin Smith, but he had to admit that he was the best platoon commander in his company and probably the battalion. His disapproval dated from when Colin Smith, fresh from Sandhurst, reported for duty in Chelsea Barracks six months earlier. Kershaw was an ambitious career officer with a perfect regimental pedigree. Both his father and grandfather had commanded the regiment, and Jeremy was determined to follow suit. After Winchester, Jeremy went up to Christchurch College, Oxford, where he earned an upper second degree in PPE, narrowly missing a first.

Colin's background could hardly have been more different. None of his family members had ever served in the Army let alone in a smart Guards regiment. His father, Bryan, had done his National Service in the RAF as a mechanic, and this experience led to him running a small garage and repair business in Reading, Colin's hometown. His mother, Daphne, was an accountant working for a Reading firm of chartered accountants who audited Bryan's garage business. Their business relationship soon turned into a loving one, and the couple decided to marry and start a family. Daphne left the firm of accountants and ran the books for her husband's business while raising first Colin and then his younger sister, Sarah.

He was not expecting an easy interview, and he was not disappointed.

"So what the hell happened out there, Colin?" Jeremy began.

"We were shot at," Colin replied lamely.

"I can see you were bloody shot at! Guardsman Pierce is lying in Musgrave Park with two Armalite rounds in his shoulder." Jeremy was angry and when angry, he started to spit whenever he spoke.

"How is Pierce doing, Jeremy?"

"Still in intensive care. Look. Why were your weapons ready when you made contact?"

Colin began to see what Jeremy was worried about. It was not just that Pierce was fighting for his life in the hospital. In Northern Ireland, the rules of engagement were very strict and governed by the Yellow Card, which every soldier had to carry. One rule stipulated that weapons should, of course, be loaded but not cocked or made ready unless engaged in a gunfight with the Provos. Colin could claim fairly that he was right to make 'weapons ready' when he heard the loud bang, but he could be criticised for 'not making safe' once he knew the bang was only a car backfiring. If he was open to criticism, then Jeremy would also be under scrutiny.

Jeremy was so ambitious and anxious that he avoided any major criticism during his two-year term as the company commander. Although Colin would take the blame for having his weapons ready as his patrol walked down Colinward Street, some of the blame might stick with Jeremy, his company commander.

Colin tried to calm things down. "We were ready earlier when we heard the explosion."

"It was only a car backfiring."

"I know, Jeremy, but I thought it was a bomb or an IED."

"Well, the military police are waiting to interview you," Jeremy replied testily. "Go and see them now."

On that note, Colin left Jeremy's office, wondering, not for the first time, why he had joined the Army in the first place.

Chapter Two

Brendan Flynn fired two rounds at the British patrol and saw that he had hit one of them. He was aiming again when one of the patrol, possibly the officer in charge, returned fire quicker than he was expecting. This threw Flynn off his shot, so he crawled back to the rear of the room, where his brother Patrick laid on guard, ready to help.

"Come on, Pat!" said Flynn urgently. "Let's get out of here."

Flynn shook his brother roughly. *He surely couldn't have nodded off*, thought Flynn before noticing that Pat's coat and trousers were wet. "That bastard British officer! He's shot! My brother!"

Flynn heaved his brother to his feet and onto his back. Flynn was over six feet tall and was built like a heavyweight boxer. Flynn lifted weights at the Ballycolman gym in Strabane and carried Pat easily down the short staircase to the rear entrance, where a car with the engine running was parked outside. They had practised the escape plan several times before the actual ambush. Flynn did not recognise the volunteer waiting impatiently behind the wheel, and as soon as Flynn had bundled Pat and himself into the rear seat with the two Armalites, the car drove off. No one spoke, but Pat groaned with every gear change.

Less than two minutes later, the car stopped on a deserted side street in Clonard. In the darkness, another volunteer, whom Flynn did not recognise, knocked on the rear door and grabbed the two Armalites and ammunition before disappearing into the night without saying a word. The car drove off again with still no word from the driver. After what seemed like another five minutes, the car stopped again, and the driver spoke for the first time.

"Get out! Now!" hissed the driver.

At the same time, the two rear doors were flung open.

Suddenly, two figures appeared, one at each rear door. This time, they spoke.

"Get out both of you now!" Flynn recognised Ciaran's rat-like features, as well as Liam's squat frame. Both Ciaran and Liam had acted as liaison officers between the IRA Belfast Brigade and the Tyrone Brigade based in Strabane, Flynn's home town.

"Pat's been shot! He needs help now!" Flynn replied.

"We'll take care of him, but you've got to move now for God's sake," urged Ciaran. At the same time, Liam grabbed Pat from the other rear door and dragged him onto the street.

"For pity's sake, be careful of him," said Flynn as Pat groaned in agony. Flynn got out of the car and went round to help Pat. Then Flynn noticed another car parked a few yards away. Ciaran and Liam bundled Flynn and Pat into the rear seat of the new car, then climbed into the front seats. From the shadows, two young girls approached the car. They both jostled into the rear seats, one on each side of Flynn and Pat, so that the two brothers were sitting in the middle.

Flynn noticed that both girls were dressed up as if for a night out. The girls smelled of cheap scents. The girl next to Flynn sprayed more scent on the four passengers in the back before the car drove off into the night.

Brendan Flynn did not know Belfast well enough to follow the route exactly. There were a lot of small side streets, turning from one to another in semi-darkness. At one point, they drove north up the West Circular, with Protestant housing estates on each side of the road. This was a dangerous time for the getaway car, outside of the relative safety of the Falls or Springfield Road. But they were well prepared. The driver knew the way and drove carefully. At one point, the car was stopped by a British Army patrol who had set up an impromptu vehicle checkpoint at the northern end of the West Circular Road. The two girls on the back seat knew what to do; they loosened their clothing, showing plenty of cleavage, and started to giggle and kiss both Flynn and Pat, making it difficult to see who was who in the rear of the car.

The Army patrol looked cold and tired. Liam, who was driving, explained.

"They've all had a good night out in the back. It's my turn to stay sober and act like a taxi."

The Army patrol commander sent the car's registration number in via his radio. But this had been expected, and both the car and its driver were clean, with no criminal records or links to the IRA. This had all been arranged in the weeks before the ambush.

After the West Circular Road, the car resumed its process of multiple turnings left and right. Pat had been groaning the entire time.

"How much further?" asked Flynn.

"Not long now," replied Liam, who looked anxiously at Pat in his rear-view mirror. By now, the graffiti on the streets was more welcoming for the getaway car, with 'Brits Out' or 'Remember Bloody Sunday' painted in large letters on the street corners. Flynn assumed they were now in the Ardoyne, a Republican estate in North Belfast. The car eventually pulled up on a quiet street, and everyone left and headed towards a small, neat, detached house set back from the road.

Immediately, the girls started laughing again, resuming the pretence of a party returning home after a good night out. However, once inside the house, the mood changed immediately to one of intense anxiety and fear.

Flynn was worried for his brother. "Pat needs help; he's been shot by the fucking Brits!"

"Bring him in here," said a quiet voice from inside the house. Flynn noticed a man standing at the back of the house's small hall. He appeared to be in his fifties or sixties with grey hair that was thinning.

"Who are you?" asked Flynn.

"Ryan Collins," he replied, "and I'm a doctor."

Ryan Collins had retired from medicine only a year earlier. He had spent ten years as a surgeon working in intensive care in the RVH. For the last five years before retirement, he had treated both wounded IRA gunmen and British soldiers. Ryan, a Roman Catholic with Republican sympathies, had distanced himself from politics. He and his family were able to afford a comfortable house in the well-to-do Holywood district of East Belfast from where violence and politics seemed remote for some of the time. But two years ago, Ulster Volunteer Force gunmen attacked a pub in Newry, killing five people, including Ryan's wife and teenage son, who had been visiting family. The senseless attack changed Ryan overnight, who, through friends and friends of friends, let it be known that he was prepared to help the IRA if asked. Since then, without warning, he had been told to report to various addresses in West Belfast, making sure he brought his doctor's bag with him. Initially, his patients suffered only minor injuries from plastic bullets or baton blows during a riot. However, after a while, he was required to treat gunshot wounds and needed a makeshift operating theatre such as the one in the back room of the house in Ardoyne.

"Help me lift him up here," said Ryan to Flynn, indicating a narrow bed. "Now, go get some rest and tell those two girls that I need them in here right away."

Flynn went out to the front room and found the two girls and Ciaran, but no Liam.

"Where's Liam?" asked Flynn.

"He's left," Ciaran replied. "We need to talk."

Flynn pretended not to hear, then sat down. He nodded to the girls. "The doctor wants you both now."

One of the girls shrugged, but they both got to their feet and quickly left the room, closing the door behind them.

Now it was just Flynn and Ciaran in the small room. After a minute, Ciaran said, "Don't worry about those two." He was referring to the girls who had just left. "They completed their nursing training at the RVH. Your brother is in good hands."

Flynn was not convinced. "What do you want to talk about?"

"Tonight. What happened?"

"I shot a Brit bastard, as we planned."

"Why only one Brit?"

Flynn felt he was being got at. "One of the Brits, who might have been their officer, fired back at us. He got Pat, the bastard."

Ciaran looked at Flynn closely. "The council won't be pleased. They wanted at least two dead Brits. That's why you two were brought up from Strabane."

"We were dead on, because no one in the bloody Belfast Brigade was up for the job."

There was a knock on the door, and one of the girls turned her head.

"What do you want, Saraid?" Ciaran demanded roughly. "We were having a talk in private."

"The doctor says he doesn't need both of us all night," Saraid replied. "So, Chloe can go home if that's OK?"

"Oh, all right, I'll give her a lift home."

He turned to Flynn. "Get some sleep. I'll be back in the morning. We can talk then."

Flynn did as he was told, and he went upstairs to find a bed. There was a small room off the landing with a double bed inside that was not taken. There was no light in the room. Flynn took off his boots, lay on the bed and was instantly asleep.

Later in the night, the silent shape of Saraid entered the room. Without fully waking Flynn, she undressed him before arranging some bedclothes over his sleeping body. Then Saraid also undressed, left her clothes on the bedroom floor and climbed into the bed beside Flynn.

Chapter Three

"Do you have any plans for post-op leave, Colin?" asked Johnny Keynsham. "I'm thinking of going skiing."

"Haven't really thought about it, Johnny; still some time to go before this bloody tour ends."

"Why not come skiing then? Something to look forward to. Spend some of the money we've saved stuck in Belfast."

Colin Smith and Johnny Keynsham were sitting in the Officers' Mess at their company base, near Springfield Road. Johnny – or Viscount Keynsham, to give him his full title – was Colin's best friend in the regiment, and they spent whatever time they could when not on patrol putting the world to rights. Jeremy had been ordered to attend a meeting at Battalion Headquarters that should keep him busy so they could relax for a while.

The Officers' Mess consisted of one unremarkable room, a few doors down from the Ops room and Jeremy's office. A few rather battered armchairs formed a semi-circle around a television at one end of the room and a table at the other end, where the officers got their meals from the cookhouse. Some regimental prints were placed on the walls in an effort to make the mess feel more like the grander one in Chelsea.

Colin thought he might like to go skiing with Johnny, and it was true he had saved some money while in Belfast. Nevertheless, he was not sure how expensive the ski holiday might end up being. Johnny's pockets were much deeper than Colin's, despite the small income from his late father's estate that supplemented his Army pay.

Colin decided to probe a little. "Who else is going, Johnny?"

"Not sure yet. Wanted to see if you were keen first."

"I'm flattered. Anyone from the regiment?"

"George and maybe Iain Munro if he can tear himself away from Scotland."

Colin liked George Simcott, who was currently on duty in the Ops Room. He was less sure about Munro – stationed with the other battalion in Windsor – who enjoyed mocking Colin about going to a grammar school. He secretly hoped he would stay on the family estate in Perthshire.

"So, just the four of us, then?" Colin asked.

"Don't be silly!" Johnny laughed. "We'll need a few girls. I'm going to ask my two bossy sisters. They'll love it if you're with us. Miranda has a crush on you. Come to think of it, Georgina has as well."

Colin felt himself blushing. Johnny was referring to Lady Miranda and Lady Georgina Keynsham, his two twin sisters, both older than Johnny, who both lived life to the full with the smart and fast set in London.

Colin was almost relieved when the door opened, and George put his head around it.

"Jeremy has just rung from Battalion Headquarters," said George. "He wants to see you, Colin, as soon as he gets back."

With that, George left abruptly and closed the door behind him.

All thoughts of ski trips vanished instantly. "Sounds like I'm in Jeremy's bad books again." sighed Colin.

"You've done nothing wrong, Colin. It's just that Jeremy doesn't know how to deal with you. If you'd been to Eton like me, he'd love you. You shot and wounded an IRA terrorist, for heaven's sake. No one else in the battalion has done that on this tour."

Colin was thankful to his friend Johnny for trying to reassure him, but he doubted that Jeremy would ever love him. After the shooting attack on Colinward Street, the whole area had been searched thoroughly. Specialist Royal Engineer search teams had been called in to assist. Colin was very worried that nothing would be found and that all the effort would have been wasted. Colin still felt that Jeremy blamed him for firing into that dark window without a clear target, and the military police had given Colin a grilling for good measure. However, just as all the search teams were winding down and getting ready to return to their bases, Sergeant Appleby announced on the net that he had spotted what looked like blood. The blood was just outside the search area at the end of an alleyway, and Sergeant Appleby had spotted this on his way back to his land rover. The RUC Scene of Crimes officer took samples away for analysis and later confirmed it was human blood.

Colin was still anxious about his meeting with Jeremy, so he waited outside his office to await his return. Colin did not have long to wait, and Jeremy arrived in a hurry at his office with a face that looked like thunder.

"Get your platoon ready to move immediately," Jeremy ordered abruptly. "You're going to Ardoyne, where the Gunners need some support. O Group in ten minutes."

Jeremy turned away, making it clear that this was all the information he was prepared to give until the O Group, short for Orders Group, when all detailed instructions would be issued.

The day following Colin and Johnny's discussion about their ski holiday, two miles north from where they had been sitting, Mary was putting the finishing touches to a letter. It was an important letter, and she wanted to deliver it to a post office as soon as possible. She cleared away her writing paper, put on her coat, grabbed the letter and prepared to leave the house that she shared with two other girls in Alliance Avenue, on the edge of the Ardoyne. Mary wanted to avoid telling her flatmates where she was going. Nothing was private in West Belfast, and sending a letter to London was unusual and would be noted. With the letter safely in her pocket, she rushed out onto the street, shouting, "Running late; see you later!"

Mary was a nurse at the RVH and her two housemates had also been trained there. She liked them both, but she had doubts about some of their friends, some of whom were probably members of the IRA. Saraid and Chloe kept unusual hours and would sometimes arrive back at the house in the middle of the night. Mary came from Strabane and was both Roman Catholic and a Republican, but she did not want to join a violent and illegal organisation. Instead, she wanted to pursue her own career while she still had the chance.

Mary walked quickly along Alliance Avenue towards Ardoyne Road. She looked over her shoulder a couple of times to check that no one she knew was following her. She was so excited. The letter she needed to post was in reply to an offer from Imperial London to read medicine. This was such good news! It meant she was going to be a doctor, train in London and be independent. Just before Ardoyne Road, there was a small grocer that was still trading, and Mary went inside. There was one loaf of bread left on the thinly stocked shelves, and Mary decided to buy it for their house, although, in truth, it was Saraid's turn to do the shopping. With the prospects of her new career turning over in her mind, she nearly forgot to pay for the loaf of bread before leaving the shop. She realised she must ring home soon, tell her mum in Strabane, and tell her two brothers. There was no phone at their house, so she needed a public phone box – one that worked – not something easy to find in West Belfast. She might even take a bus to the city centre and telephone from there.

She left the shop with her head filled with thoughts about her future. A car was parked outside the shop with the engine running. Moments after leaving the store, a loud explosion ripped through the air, tearing the small shop to pieces. Mary was flown sideways by the blast and lay unconscious a few yards from the shop, which was now a burning wreck. The fire spread rapidly from the shop to the adjacent buildings in the street, and it was already intense.

On the other side of the street, Colin had just arrived with his platoon. They had been summoned to Alliance Avenue to investigate the sighting of a stolen car, which might have caused the explosion. Colin could see a young girl with blonde hair lying on the street a yard in front of a house that was adjacent to the shop that was now completely destroyed. Lumps of masonry, burning timber and glass were landing on the street, very close to the girl who was clearly still unconscious. The fire service had just arrived and was already stopping anyone approaching the ablaze buildings, which were a danger to everyone.

Colin realised that no one could see Mary, who was hidden by all the smoke billowing across the street. Colin knew he should secure the area, stand back and let the fire crew perform their dangerous job.

Perhaps it was all the frustration of the past few weeks and his constant difficulties with Jeremy that made Colin ignore the cordon and run into the middle of the smoke, where he thought he could find the girl. At first, Colin's platoon sergeant tried to intervene and shouted a warning, but Colin had already run into the thick black smoke. Colin had only run a few feet into the smoke before he started coughing and choking. It was also very difficult to see, and his eyes were stinging as if he were in a CS gas chamber. He found it very difficult to find where the young girl was lying, and it almost came as a relief when he tripped over her motionless body. Although she was not heavy, it was very difficult to lift her as well as keep hold of his rifle, which was still attached to his wrist. After trying and failing to carry her in a fireman's lift, Colin decided to drag her out of the smoke using his rifle as a sort of prop, with it placed across the girl's body under her chin and one of Colin's hands on each end of the rifle. In this awkward position, Colin started to stagger out of the smoke. Progress was very slow, and the smoke was so thick that Colin was not even sure he was moving in the right direction. By now, he was finding it impossible to breathe, and his body felt very hot. After a few more steps, Colin could no longer stand, and, losing consciousness, he slumped to the ground.

Chapter Four

The Royal Victoria Hospital, or the Royal as it is known by many, lies in the Falls Road, where it forms a crossroads with the Springfield and Grosvenor roads. Situated in the heart of West Belfast, it has treated both Catholic and Protestant patients since it moved to its present location in 1903.

Early in the morning, after the bomb attack in Ardoyne, Sister Kath O'Rourke, Head of Nursing at the Intensive Care Unit, was doing her rounds. She looked at the handsome young man lying unconscious on the hospital bed and listened to Nurse Donovan's report. He looked thin, and there were lines around his blue eyes that were still half closed, suggesting too much stress in one so young. He was badly bruised all over his arms and shoulders, and his breathing was still weak. He could not breathe properly without a ventilator when he arrived in an ambulance at the Royal the day before. Despite this, there were no broken bones, and a full recovery was likely in time.

"Thank you, Nurse Donovan," said Sister Kath when she had finished listening to the report. "Let's hope we can move him to a ward later today. He's a good-looking lad."

"Not bad at all," replied Nurse Donovan who, after a pause, added, "for a Brit."

Sister Kath O'Rourke turned quickly to look Nurse Donovan straight in the eyes. "They're all our patients, Nurse, no matter who they are." Her tone was sharper than a razor blade. Nurse Donovan mumbled an apology. She was new to the RVH and had not fully grasped the three rules that applied: be fair to everyone, listen to everyone and, above all, obey Sister Kath without question.

"Now, how is dear Mary doing?" asked Sister Kath.

They both turned their attention to another bed a few feet away, where a young girl with bright blonde hair was asleep. Sister Kath liked Mary, or Nurse Mary, as she was called at work. She was one of her best nurses in intensive care and had a bright future. She looked so frail lying in a ward where, only three days ago, she had been the nurse on duty, not the patient. She listened carefully to Nurse Donovan's report and was relieved to hear that she should also be well enough to move out of intensive care later today.

Sister Kath had heard about the Ardoyne bombing on Downtown Radio that morning and how a young girl had been rescued by a British soldier from a fire. No names had been mentioned, but everyone in the Royal knew that one of their nurses was now lying in intensive care beside the Brit who had rescued her.

Following the bombing, his friend Johnny Keynsham was the first person to arrive at the Royal, anxious to see Colin. Johnny had been on duty in the Ops Room and had taken the telephone call from the Gunners in the Ardoyne with the shocking news that Colin was injured. Johnny immediately sent a runner to alert Jeremy, who had burst into the Ops Room from his office. He had snatched the telephone receiver from Johnny. There followed a tense conversation in which Jeremy demanded to speak to the Gunner battery commander, Major John Saunders, in order to obtain a full report. This was very awkward; Jeremy had no right to make demands on another officer of equal rank. However, the warrant officer on duty handled the situation tactfully, explaining that Major Saunders was not able to speak as he was on the ground dealing with the aftermath of the incident. The only information available was that Colin was on his way to the RVH. Johnny immediately volunteered to go to the RVH without delay, and Jeremy readily agreed, but not before demanding frequent reports on the situation.

It was agreed that Johnny would attract less attention if he visited the RVH in civilian clothes. He travelled there in the back of a lightly armoured vehicle known as a pig by the Army. These pigs had no weaponry but offered some protection against small arms fire. Nevertheless, pigs were sometimes labelled tanks by the residents of West Belfast. Johnny was dropped at the front entrance of the RVH, and, with a 9mm pistol hidden inside his jacket, he set about looking for his friend.

Johnny found his way to the intensive care ward and asked to see Colin Smith. He was told to wait but, after a while, still worried, he asked again to see his friend, becoming a little angry. Shortly afterwards, a formidable-looking lady appeared and introduced herself to Johnny as Sister Kath O'Rourke. She explained firmly that there was no question of seeing Colin until he was stronger.

"But will he be all right?" Johnny asked anxiously. Kath could see that the young man standing before her was very worried, and her expression softened.

"Why don't we pop along to the canteen together and have a cup of tea?" Kath suggested. Johnny was so surprised by an offer of a cup of tea that he stood there speechless. Sister Kath took him by the arm and guided him down a staircase to a busy canteen. Johnny was glad to be in civilian clothes. There was a long queue of nurses and doctors waiting to be served, and they took up positions at the back of the line. Johnny expected a long wait, but the sight of Sister Kath made the queue shorten in front of them, and they were soon served their cups of tea. Kath led Johnny over to a table where four young nurses were seated, and they took the two remaining places at the table. Kath's arrival had the effect of making the nurses finish their tea quickly and return to their duties. The canteen was nearly empty now, and they were able to have a quiet chat.

Sister Kath explained that Colin should make a full recovery and that what he needed now was rest. She also said, both gently and firmly, that Colin could not be visited by anyone until the consultant had seen him again and that Johnny would just have to wait until then.

After his tea, during which Johnny learnt a great deal about Sister Kath's childhood and her seven siblings in the Markets area of West Belfast, he found a call box and rang his company base to report. He learned that Jeremy had set off for Ardoyne to see the site of the bomb attack and was told to remain at the RVH and ring again after another hour. As a result, Johnny could do nothing but find a chair in the waiting room and wait for news about his friend.

As Johnny sat waiting to see his friend, his thoughts wandered to when he first met Colin at the Royal Military Academy Sandhurst. They had been put in the same platoon and were often paired together. It was obvious from the start of the course that Colin was a very capable officer cadet.

The first few weeks at Sandhurst were hard, and you were never allowed to relax from the moment you woke at five a.m. until you collapsed on the floor of your bunk at midnight. Your bunk, or small room, had to be immaculate at all times, and Johnny remembered sleeping on the floor so as not to mess up his bed that would be inspected at five a.m. While Johnny was naturally untidy and a little scruffy for a potential Guards officer, Colin seemed to find it easy to keep his room tidy and be smart on parade.

With family connections to the Brigade of Guards, Johnny's future lay with a Guards regiment, subject to him passing Sandhurst. Colin's position was very different. With no strong links to the Army, he had to find a regiment that would offer him a place, and this was a competitive process. Perhaps it was the different backgrounds that led the directing staff at Sandhurst to pair Johnny and Colin together. Johnny remembered a night navigation exercise on Barossa Common where nearly all the officer cadets were hopelessly lost, but somehow Colin found his way around the course so that he and Johnny were the first pair to complete the exercise. Johnny had difficulty keeping his equipment secure, and on one occasion even mislaid his rifle during an exercise, for which the penalty would have been very severe if discovered. Colin could easily have left Johnny to try and find his rifle and complete his own route march in record time but, instead, he gave up his run in order to help Johnny. Both Johnny and Colin were last to complete the course, but they found Johnny's rifle with minutes to spare.

Although Johnny owed a great deal to Colin, he was too modest to realise how much he had helped his friend in return. Colin had always wanted to join the Army since childhood, but he had no idea about the regimental system that made the British Army unique. Without patronising his friend, Johnny introduced him to his friends on the course, most of them from public schools and who were also destined for smart regiments in the Guards or the Cavalry.

Johnny was suddenly brought back to the present when a very tall and strong-looking man sat down in the seat beside him. The row of chairs shook with the force of him trying to make himself comfortable on the small seat. The man did not sit for long, and he almost sprang out of his chair with remarkable agility for such a massive man and approached a nurse who had just entered the waiting room.

"Are you in charge here?" he demanded aggressively.

"My name is Nurse Donovan, and I am one of the nurses on this ward," she replied warily. "How can I help?"

"I've come to see my sister. I want to see her now," demanded the man roughly.

"I shall have to check with Sister. Please take a seat."

"I don't want to sit, woman!" he was now speaking loudly.

Johnny couldn't help himself and said, "I'm waiting as well, you know."

The sound of Johnny's English accent angered the man.

"No one asked you, you British bastard; who are you anyway?" He took a step towards Johnny, who began to feel very vulnerable.

Fortunately, Sister Kath appeared from nowhere and immediately confronted the man.

"There's no need for that sort of language here. Take a seat here and let me know what's up."

He grudgingly sat down. Sister Kath sat down beside him and started talking. Johnny moved away so as not to intrude on their conversation. He noted there was a stern look in her eyes, and she looked very different from the Kath who had bought him a cup of tea earlier.

After a short conversation, both Sister Kath and the man stood up and Johnny was relieved to see him leave the waiting room. Then Sister Kath came over to sit by Johnny and her face relaxed a little.

"I've just heard that your friend has regained consciousness. He is being moved to Alexandria ward; give it a few hours and you can visit him."

"Thanks," Johnny replied, "I'll do that. By the way, who was that big fellow with the temper?"

"His name is Brendan Flynn and he's the brother of the wee girl your friend rescued. You'd do well to stay out of his way."

Chapter Five

Mary stood naked in the lecture hall at Imperial College, London. On the dais in front of her, the senior tutors were sitting on thrones, asking why she had not written to them. Then the lecture hall burst into flames, and someone was nudging her shoulder.

When she woke up from her dream, she realised that her brother Brendan was sitting beside her bed with an anxious look on his face.

"The doctor says you are going to be OK," said Brendan. "You need to rest, though."

"Mum?" Mary mumbled, not yet realising where she was.

"I've spoken to Mum, she knows you're in hospital. She wants to come and see you, but she has to stay with Pat."

"Pat?" Mary whispered and then closed her eyes in sleep.

Brendan Flynn realised with a jolt that Mary, of course, knew nothing about Pat's wounding two weeks earlier. The shooting attack on the British patrol in Colinward Street had been planned in total secrecy. Even Brendan and Pat's presence in Belfast was known only to a few in the IRA's Belfast Brigade.

Brendan watched Mary sleep, and his thoughts returned to that night, Pat's wounding, and their escape across Belfast to the small house in the Ardoyne. Brendan had stayed holed up in the Ardoyne house for three days after the shooting. Ciaran returned just once, but said nothing about the ambush other than urging Brendan and Pat to escape across the border to Dundalk as soon as Pat was well enough to travel. Fortunately, Pat was stronger after two days, and the doctor reluctantly agreed to let Pat make the journey south. Their trip to Dundalk was uneventful, and Pat was taken to a hospital used frequently by the IRA, where no questions were asked about how patients sustained their injuries. After a few days in Dundalk, Pat was moved again, this time to a small hospital in Letterkenny, taking the long route around via Sligo avoiding the north. Pat was still weak and was likely to stay in Letterkenny for some time, close to Strabane over the border where Pat's mother lived alone in the Ballycolman Estate.

After a short while, Mary opened her eyes again to see Brendan still sitting beside the bed, looking uncomfortable.

"What's this about, Pat?" Mary asked.

"He had an accident," Brendan lied. He spoke softly, not wanting the ward to hear the details. "Mum is looking after him. Can I get you some things from the shops?" added Brendan, anxious to change the subject.

But Mary had fallen asleep again, and Brendan was anxious to leave the RVH where he had already drawn too much attention to himself. He decided to leave the ward and go outside.

On his way to the exit, he saw the young man with the British accent who had spoken to him while waiting for Mary to recover. He decided to follow him to see who he was, and his suspicions proved to be correct when he saw the man climb into the back of an army pig outside the main entrance in Grosvenor Road.

Over the next week, Mary grew stronger and was able to walk around the ward a little. There was a small canteen along the corridor from her ward, which was shared with patients from other wards who were strong enough to walk. She had heard nothing more from Brendan and at times wondered if she had dreamt of his short visit. She had received a short letter from her mother in Strabane, but it contained little information about either Pat or Brendan. She wanted to tell her mother about her plans for the future, but this was not easy.

Mary wondered if the offer from Imperial in London to study medicine was all a dream. The bombing attack, her injuries and waking up in the RVH had made it very difficult to remember what had happened in the minutes before the attack. She had asked to see her belongings, which were brought to her in a pitifully small plastic bag. She had left her house with nothing except the clothes she was wearing, and these were now badly burnt and torn. There was no sign of her letter to Imperial, and she was worried that she would lose her place on the course if she didn't respond. Her application papers were in her room at the house in Ardoyne and Mary wondered if either Saraid or Chloe could bring them to her when they came to visit her. However, she had not mentioned her plans to leave Belfast and go to London to her housemates. She was wary of telling them too much.

There was a pay phone just outside the canteen where she had tried to telephone her mother, but there had been no answer. There was always a queue of noisy patients waiting to use the phone and there was little privacy. Nevertheless, Mary was getting increasingly anxious about the possibility of her losing her place, so she decided to try the university in London again. She was allowed one hour of walking to and from the ward and the canteen and on her next walkabout, she joined the queue where she found there were three patients ahead of her. The minutes went by, and Mary became anxious that her whole hour would vanish before even reaching the phone. Soon a queue of people formed behind her, some of whom she recognised from her ward, and they were all becoming agitated as well as the minutes ticked by.

The only person who seemed unconcerned about the delay despite being at the back of the queue was a young man who Mary did not recognise.

Eventually, it was Mary's turn. She rang 192 for directory inquiries and asked for Imperial University's telephone number. Mary was not familiar with using a public telephone, and there was still a lot of noise in the corridor. She noticed that the handsome man was now next in the queue, and the others had given up waiting. The operator asked Mary which department she wanted, and she opted for admissions before being put through directly. After a few rings, an English voice asked how she could help, and at the same time, the pips started on the phone asking for cash. Mary fumbled with the cash she had prepared and managed to insert a 10-pence piece into the slot on the side of the phone. Then she started to explain in a rush that she had received a letter offering a place to read medicine but then, disaster, the pips started again! Mary was flustered and dropped her change, 10 pence pieces rolling along the corridor like the wheels from a broken bus. At her side, a quiet voice spoke calmly. "Try these. Here, let me help." It was the man she saw earlier and, without delay, he pushed a few coins into the slot. Mary tried to mumble a thank you, but the man said, "Go on, make your call; it sounds important." Somewhat reassured by the help of the kind stranger, she managed to explain that she had received a letter from the university offering a place but had not been able to reply. Whenever the pips resumed, the kind stranger put more coins in the slot.

"I live in Ardoyne, Belfast. There was a bomb attack, and I was injured. My letter was destroyed…"

The kind stranger looked at Mary with a puzzled expression.

The English operator told Mary not to worry and another letter would be sent out to her shortly. Mary put down the handset, much happier than before. She turned to say a thank you to her kind stranger, but he had already left her, presumably to return to his ward.

Chapter Six

Colin shuffled up and down the corridor outside his ward. He found he could now walk without crutches and his breathing was getting stronger.

He knew every step of the way. For a change, he would sometimes walk to the canteen, passing the telephone where he had helped the pretty blonde girl yesterday. He wondered if she had realised that it was he who had dragged her to safety in the Ardoyne. He stopped walking for a moment and peered through a window at the end of the corridor. Everything was spotless inside but on the outside, the glass was grimy and difficult to see through. Nevertheless, he could make out the Falls Road and Springfield Road junctions. Colin had deployed there with his platoon only a month earlier to deal with riots in protest at the death of an IRA hunger striker. He remembered the night clearly and he felt vulnerable being so close to the scene, dressed only in his hospital gown with no weapon for protection.

It was time to return to his ward and bed. His short walk had tired him, and it would be a relief to lie down again. He glanced at his Army watch, a G1098 to replace his watch that had been destroyed in the fire and noted that Johnny was due to visit him later. He had had a few visitors, as well as Johnny, since being admitted to the RVH. These included his commanding officer and the Gunner battery commander, who said that Colin's actions had helped restore some goodwill in the Ardoyne. Jeremy had also come to see him, but his visit was less welcome. He criticised his decision to run headlong into a fire to rescue a civilian, and his injuries and admission to the RVH had left him short of staff back at the base.

Colin climbed back into bed in his ward. A few nurses were standing around talking to each other and some of the patients. Colin wondered if there was even a hint of romance in the air. Then the swing doors at the end of the ward opened suddenly and Sister Kath O'Rourke marched into the middle. The nurses who had been gossiping now became very busy and one even left the ward.

"Wait a moment, nurses!" said Sister Kath loudly. "I'm here to remind you that there's a show in our theatre in half an hour. I want to see plenty of nurses with those patients who are well enough at the show. Nurse Donovan has a few tickets."

Nurse Donovan started walking around the ward, dispensing tickets and collecting money for charity. Meanwhile, Sister Kath walked over to Colin's bed and said quietly, "We are all very thankful for what you did. Mary is very popular here."

"Mary?" said Colin.

"The wee girl you rescued in the Ardoyne, of course! She wants to say thank you to you in person, but she's a shy girl. Come to the show this afternoon and you can have a chat."

Sister Kath then described Mary as a nurse in more detail and explained how she was highly thought of. Colin did not mention his brief telephone meeting with the blonde girl, whose name he now knew to be Mary. He also avoided blurting out that, according to what he heard Mary say on the telephone, it was likely that Mary would be leaving Belfast for London.

Their conversation came to an end with Johnny Keynsham's arrival and Sister Kath left the two young men to speak in peace. Johnny was in civilian clothes, and as he sat down, he took off his jacket, dropping it on the floor of the ward with a loud thud. Colin guessed it was his 9mm Browning pistol that made the sound. Johnny brought news that Colin was going to be transferred to Musgrave Park, a military hospital, in a safer part of Belfast. Colin would be sorry to leave the RVH. He liked the slightly chaotic atmosphere, the overworked nurses who never seemed to lose their sense of humour and the fact that he had started to bond with some of the other patients. He had been to Musgrave Park only once to visit Guardsman Pierce, who was still recovering from his gunshot wounds. Pierce was a natural rebel and disliked the strict regime of a military hospital. He had told Colin, only half-jokingly, that when an officer visited the ward, you had to lie in your bed as if standing to attention.

"Sorry, Colin," said Johnny, "you've got to move. It's too dangerous here, and anyway, Jeremy insists. A pig will be here tomorrow at 0900."

Colin and Johnny would have chatted for longer, but Sister Kath announced loudly that it was time to move to the theatre for the show. Johnny grabbed his jacket and made his way to leave the ward.

"I'll come and visit you at Musgrave, Colin."

Once Johnny had left, Colin started to climb out of bed. His legs were still stiff and sore, so it took him a few moments to sit up and swing his legs down to the floor of the ward. As his feet touched the floor, he felt something cold against the sole of his right foot. When Colin looked down, he saw that his feet were on top of Johnny's 9mm pistol, which must have fallen out of his jacket in his rush to leave.

"Bloody hell, Johnny!" Colin swore quietly. "Why can't you keep hold of your kit?" Colin thought quickly about what he should do. He couldn't just leave the pistol in the ward while he went to the show. He couldn't hand the pistol to a nurse for safekeeping. He'd have to take the pistol with him to the show!

Everyone was now making their way to the theatre. They were a strange group that shuffled along the corridor to the main lift that would take them down two floors to the theatre. Some were in wheelchairs, and some were on crutches. Colin had just dispensed with his crutches and could walk unaided, albeit slowly. Amongst them were nurses from the ward and other wards. Colin spotted both

Sister Kath and Nurse Donovan, and it seemed as if most of the hospital was heading in the same direction.

Colin had worn an extra gown, not because he was cold, but because he needed extra clothing to hide the pistol. It was awkward carrying the weapon and Colin was worried that he would drop it and cause an incident.

When they reached the venue, Colin was surprised to see that it appeared to be a properly fitted theatre with a stage, curtains and lights.

"Come and sit over here," said the unmistakable voice of Sister Kath and, like everyone else in the RVH, Colin did what she said and followed her to some seats at the end of a row. As expected, there was the young blonde girl, whom Colin now knew as Mary.

Sister Kath checked that they were both seated and then left them to talk.

"I wanted to say thank you for what you did," began Mary.

"That's OK. I was passing and had some coins on me," Colin replied.

There was a hint of a smile on Mary's face. "I meant saving my life in the Ardoyne."

"I just did what I thought was right. I hope you're recovering OK?"

"Yes, thanks; I should be leaving soon."

"Will you be going to London?" Colin asked. "I couldn't help hearing some of your conversation on the phone."

"I don't know yet; I want to, but I've got a lot to sort out, family things."

Their brief conversation was interrupted by the start of the show. It was a revue and a larger-than-life compère came onto the stage. He made some jokes about life in Belfast as well as introducing the various acts. One of the performers was a magician who did clever tricks with a length of rope, but he spoke with a very English accent and found it difficult to bond with his audience. The top of the bill was a singer who had painted his face dark brown and spoke with a supposed Asian accent. He sang a catchy song about the wonders of Belfast whatever the colour of your skin. The audience enjoyed this and sang along happily. Colin was also enjoying himself and looked forward to talking to Mary when the show ended. Then, Colin felt a gentle tap on his shoulder and turned to see a nurse whom he did not recognise.

"There's a man to see you at the main reception," She said.

Johnny must be here to retrieve his 9mm, Colin thought.

The nurse helped him to his feet and, with a brief apology to Mary, Colin made his way out of the auditorium. The nurse said nothing as they went up in the lift to the main reception. When the lift doors creaked open, another nurse stood waiting to greet him. She was very pretty and smiled at Colin, but her eyes were hard and cold.

"Come this way, please, Colin." She pointed to the main entrance, where a car had just pulled up outside.

Something felt very wrong. "I was expecting an army…"

Colin did not finish his sentence because he felt the cold, hard metal of a pistol ramming into his back. The nurse who had come up with him from the theatre was standing inches behind him. "Move to the car," she said. Colin could see the driver, a large man with a brutal look on his face.

The pretty nurse also turned towards the car. Colin knew, if he got into the vehicle, he would be killed.

Then, from the lift doors behind them, someone said, "Saraid, what are you doing here?" It was Mary.

Mary's question made both nurses look her way. It was all the distraction Colin needed and he shoved one of the nurses out of the way. She slipped and dropped her pistol, which went sliding along the floor of the main reception, causing people to scream.

Saraid had now also drawn a pistol. "You English bastard!" She hissed and fired, just missing Colin. Colin fumbled in his gown and found Johnny's pistol, which he cocked. Saraid was aiming again but Colin managed to fire first, hitting Saraid, who dropped to the ground. The other nurse had picked up her pistol by now and turned to fire but seeing Saraid on the floor, she lost her nerve, ran to the door and jumped into the car, which sped away.

Mary was kneeling over Saraid. Her face was white. "She's dead," she said, sobbing.

Colin went to go over to help but he couldn't because one of his legs wouldn't move. He looked down at his legs, which were covered in blood. People were screaming. No one knew what to do. Everyone was staring at Colin, who stood in the main reception area, covered in blood, still holding Johnny's pistol. An RUC constable appeared and aimed his pistol at Colin. *He thinks I'm a terrorist! He's going to shoot me!* thought Colin.

"Dear Mother of God!" Put that gun down! "He's a patient!" Sister Kath had appeared on the scene and her words were the last thing Colin heard before everything went blank.

Chapter Seven

The Army didn't wait until nine o'clock the next morning before moving Colin to Musgrave Park. In less than twenty minutes after the gunfight, Colin was placed in an army ambulance and closely protected by an armed convoy, he was driven straight to the military wing of the hospital. The exertion of being shot at by Saraid, returning fire and killing her had caused one of Colin's previous wounds to reopen, and he required immediate surgery when he arrived at Musgrave Park.

The shooting attack became a major incident and caught the attention of the senior echelons of both the Security Services and the IRA. News of the shooting was first reported on the recently created Downtown Radio, which again displayed the ability to know what was going on in Belfast before either the Army or the RUC. This did not play well for the Commander of the Land Forces at Headquarters Northern Ireland in Lisburn, who summoned his senior intelligence staff for an urgent briefing. On the other hand, for the listeners of Downtown Radio, the story had everything; a pretty nurse who turned out to be a terrorist, a shooting attack against a patient who turned out to be an Army officer, and all the action played out in the public reception hall of the RVH.

Both sides were quick to put their side of the story. The Army condemned the attempted murder of a patient in the RVH. The IRA claimed that the Army had authorised a shoot-to-kill policy using undercover soldiers in the hospital.

The Army had serious questions to answer internally. Why had Colin not been moved to the relative safety of Musgrave Park much earlier? At this point, Jeremy Kershaw had covered his position skilfully. He had pressed for Colin to be moved at the weekly Battalion O Groups, and his views had been recorded in the minutes. Johnny Keynsham found himself in big trouble over his pistol. As soon as Colin was well enough to speak, he claimed that Johnny had lent him his pistol for personal protection. Of course, no one in the battalion believed this for a moment. Johnny's reputation for mislaying his equipment was well known. However, it was also the case that if Johnny had not left his pistol at the Royal, Colin would have been murdered. As it happened, it was a mysterious terrorist who was lying dead, not Colin.

Colin spent the remaining weeks of the tour recovering in Musgrave Park. As soon as he was well enough, he was interviewed repeatedly by the military police, asking how he had the pistol, who shot at him and why he returned fire. Initially, these interviews took place beside Colin's bed but as soon as he grew stronger, he was questioned in a small office that had been requisitioned by the military police. Colin explained carefully that he had never met his attackers before, including the girl who had escaped and the driver of the getaway car. He said as little as possible about Mary and how she had distracted Saraid at a critical moment. He wanted to speak to Mary, but he had no way of contacting her without drawing attention to her role in the incident. Colin was very thankful that Saraid's pistol had been found in the reception area after the attack and upon examination, it had been fired. The spent round that had missed Colin was found in the frame of a large painting of the Langan River hanging beside the main lifts.

Musgrave Park's regime was a world apart from the Royal. Everything was very disciplined and tightly controlled and Colin missed the lively buzz that had existed in the RVH. But it was secure, and although the nurses weren't always friendly, at least they didn't shoot at their patients. One upside of Colin's new stay was his reunion with Guardsman Simon Pierce, who was now recovering quickly from his bullet wounds in Colinward Street. They spent time together, talking about the tour and chuckling about the hospital staff. These chats were very relaxed and on first-name terms, something that would be unthinkable in the battalion.

Colin decided to write to Sister Kath O'Rourke at the RVH. He wanted to thank her and her staff for looking after him so well. He also inquired about Mary and whether there was any way he could contact her. He posted the letter to Sister Kath at the RVH not certain that it would ever reach her. He wrote using his home address in

Reading, and he hoped he would receive a reply eventually.

After two weeks, both Colin and Simon Pierce had recovered sufficiently to be discharged. The battalion's tour was nearly over, and it was time to return to Chelsea Barracks in London. On Colin's last day in the hospital, as he was packing his things for the journey, he was told to report to the stuffy little office, yet again, this time to be questioned by a Captain S Matthews, Royal Military Police. He had not been questioned for a couple of days and the thought of another formal interview was depressing.

When he entered the office, a girl in an RMP uniform stood up from the desk and introduced herself as Captain Sarah Matthews. Colin was slightly taken aback. In his short time in the Army, he had not met many female officers. There had been no female officer cadets at Sandhurst, and potential officers for the Women's Royal Army Corps trained at a separate base in Camberley. Sarah Matthews was pretty in a bossy way and Colin guessed she had been a prefect at school or even Head Girl. It was a warm day and Sarah was dressed in shirt sleeve order, dispensing with her Army jumper. This showed off her shapely figure, but her shirt was a little too small and tight around her breasts. As a result, Colin's eyes drifted to her figure.

"This is Major Smith," Captain Matthews began, clearly irritated and keen to take control of the interview.

Colin looked up at a man who may have been in his late thirties or forties, and whose hair was starting to grey. He wore crowns on his shoulders to show his rank but with no stable belt or beret in sight, Colin could not tell in which regiment he served. He stood in a corner behind Captain Matthews' desk, looking carefully at Colin. He did not acknowledge the brief introduction and said nothing.

"Perhaps we're related?" Colin asked, regretting his flippancy immediately. Major Smith did not answer.

Sarah Matthews was still irritated. She fired off a series of questions at Colin, most of which he had already answered in the preceding days.

"Did you recognise the woman you shot?"

"No," Colin replied. "And she shot at me."

"And the other woman?"

"No."

"What about the driver of the getaway car?"

"No"

Then Sarah Matthews asked a new question. "How do you know Mary Flynn?"

Colin was surprised. No one had ever told him Mary's surname.

"I don't know her full name. I only know she's called Mary, and I met her for the first time when I pulled her from a fire in the Ardoyne."

Sarah Matthews persisted with her questions for a few more minutes and then suddenly finished the interview. The whole meeting had lasted less than ten minutes, and Major Smith had not uttered a word throughout.

Without the thought of returning to London uppermost in his mind, Colin might have thought this last encounter was very odd but as soon as Sarah Matthews had finished her questions, he left the interview room and set about packing up his kit for the journey home.

Colin gave no more thought to the military police and was just thankful to be leaving the province that had so nearly cost him his life.

Chapter Eight

"March off the Colour!" Major Jeremy Kershaw's voice carried clearly across Friary Court outside St James Palace in London. Colin Smith held the regimental colour to his front and marched smartly into the confines of the palace. There was a round of applause from some spectators standing along Marlborough Road, and Colin hoped that his mother and sister had been able to see the parade.

As soon as he was out of sight of the general public, he heaved a sigh of relief. The Guard Mount had gone well, including the long march from Chelsea Barracks to the forecourt of Buckingham Palace, where the new guard, commanded by Jeremy, became the Queen's Guard. Colin's mind turned to his immediate duties. He walked past the guardroom and entered a narrow alleyway. On his right was a black door with an intercom on its left. Colin pressed the buzzer, which was answered almost immediately.

"It's the Ensign," said Colin into the microphone.

The door swung open, and Colin stood at the bottom of a steep flight of stairs. He carried the colour up the stairs, making sure not to hit the ceiling. At the top of the stairs, he was met by the Mess Sergeant who had operated the intercom. Colin placed the colour in the corner of the main mess room by the telephone, then checked the details of the guests who would be arriving for lunch at one p.m. The day before, he had agreed to the menus with the Mess Sergeant on the telephone. Colin would have liked to linger in the cool comfort of the Officers' Mess, but he had duties to perform, so he went back down the stairs, opened the door to the alleyway, letting the door lock behind him, and turned left. After a few feet on his left, Colin turned left again and entered the main guardroom.

Inside the guardroom, everyone was very busy. Colin took the opportunity to remove his bearskin, which felt hot and heavy along his forehead. The guardsmen had just finished the guard mount and were now getting ready for the guard. Some were now off duty, walking around in sweatshirts, having discarded their hot tunics. Others were preparing to go on guard at the various sentry boxes dotted around St James' Palace. There was a very large mirror just inside the door of the guardroom, where several guardsmen were checking their uniforms, and Colin took the opportunity to look at his own turnout. His fair hair was damp with sweat, and there was a mark along the centre of his high forehead where his bearskin fitted his head a little too tightly. His eyes were a very light blue and they looked back at Colin curiously. Today, they sparkled as they often did when Colin was happy. His eyes turned downwards to his tunic and the Northern Ireland medal which was pinned on his chest to the left. All ranks were awarded this medal after a tour in Northern Ireland. However, on Colin's medal, there was an oak leaf in the centre to show that he had been mentioned in dispatches. This award had come as a surprise to Colin, who had been given no prior notice and he did not even know for certain what action had earned him a MID. He assumed it was his rescue of Mary in the Ardoyne, on the recommendation of Major Saunders of the Gunners.

"We're ready to go, sir." Colin turned to see Sergeant Appleby, who had been in Belfast with him. Together, they set off to inspect the sentries who were posted around St James' Palace. These included the sentry boxes in Stable Yard Road and the sentry post at the bottom of St James', facing upwards towards the clubs of Boodles and Whites, and then Mayfair beyond. As usual, a policeman was on duty in his box outside Lancaster House, where Stable Yard Road meets Ambassadors Court, and the police officer on duty waved a friendly greeting to Colin and his small squad of Guardsmen as they marched past.

At the sentry box in Stable Yard Road, Colin was pleased to see that Guardsman Simon Pierce was on duty. Pierce saluted smartly by smacking his left arm against his rifle, which he carried in his right hand. Colin hoped the movement did not cause him any pain, as two Armalite rounds had entered his right shoulder earlier in the year.

"How was the Guard Mount?" asked Colin. "And your shoulder?"

"No problems, sir," Pierce replied, "lots of pretty girls in the crowd."

Sergeant Appleby looked at Pierce suspiciously. But everything was in good order, and they carried on with their inspection of the other sentries. As soon as he had completed his rounds, Colin returned to the Officers' Mess and placed his bearskin alongside Jeremy's on the stand outside the door to the main mess room.

At lunch, three officers would be present. The Captain of the Guard, Jeremy Kershaw, the Subaltern, Johnny Keynsham and finally Colin as the Ensign. All three could invite guests of both sexes to lunch and then drinks in the evening. Guests for dinner were restricted to men only and dressed in black tie. Colin had asked his mother and sister for lunch. This was a big moment for all the family, and Colin hoped they had made the train journey from Reading in good time to see the Guard Mount.

From the landing outside the mess room, there was another steep flight of stairs to the top floor, where there were three bedrooms for each of the three officers on guard. Colin ran up the stairs and entered his room, gratefully removing his hot and heavy tunic and Wellington boots. After washing, he changed into a clean collarless white shirt, a pair of blue trousers with a large red stripe running down each leg and finally his blue uniform jacket, known as a jumper in the regiment. He checked himself in the mirror and realised that he was nervous. He hoped that Sarah and his mother would enjoy lunch at St James' and not be overwhelmed by the location and his fellow officers.

Colin left his room and bumped into Johnny Keynsham on the landing, who had just returned from the guardroom at Buckingham Palace. Although Johnny would spend most of his time on guard at St James', he would have to visit Buckingham Palace frequently and sleep there overnight. After a brief greeting, Johnny went into his room to change, and Colin headed down the top flight of stairs to the main mess room. On the first floor landing, all three bearskins were laid out on stands in a row, indicating that all three officers were present within the Officers' Mess at St James'.

When Colin entered the mess room, he found Jeremy already dressed for lunch sitting on a bum warmer in front of the fireplace. It was a very warm day, and there was no need for a fire. As always, Jeremy was dressed immaculately. As Captain of the Queen's Guard, he wore a boating jacket with regimental buttons gleaming after hours of polishing by his orderly. He wore a cream shirt with a freshly ironed 'blue, red, blue' Brigade of Guards tie. The cuffs of his shirt protruded from the sleeves of his boating jacket just enough to show off the regimental cufflinks that had been made to order by Cartier. An aroma suggesting an expensive lotion from either Curzon or Jermyn Street wafted towards Colin's position.

"Remind me," Jeremy drawled, "who have you invited for lunch?"

Jeremy knew perfectly well that Colin had asked his mother and sister for lunch. He also knew that these were Colin's first guests ever on Queens Guard and that, for him, it was a big occasion. But, before Colin could answer, Johnny Keynsham appeared.

"Sorry, I'm late!" said Johnny, slightly out of breath. "Couldn't find my cufflinks. Colin, I borrowed a pair from you. I hope that's OK?"

Colin didn't mind and was about to answer Jeremy's question when a quiet voice behind him whispered. "Hello, Colin, dear."

Colin turned to find his mother and his sister standing before him. "Did you find the way, Mum?" Colin asked before kissing both his mother and sister.

"Of course, a very charming man called Simon Pierce helped us on our way and told us how pretty we both looked in our dresses!" Colin couldn't help but smile. He would have to speak to Guardsman Pierce later about chatting with members of the public, but he was right; both his mother and sister did look lovely.

"Jeremy, may I introduce my mother, Daphne, and my sister, Sarah?"

"How do you do?" said Jeremy formally. "Did you have a good journey from Reading?"

"Yes, thanks," Daphne replied. "We came up first thing and spent the morning in London."

"Some shopping, perhaps?" Jeremy asked.

"No, we went to see Imperial. Sarah wants to go there to read medicine."

"And is Imperial best for medicine?" Jeremy enquired.

"Oh, yes!" Sarah entered the conversation. "Mum wants me to go to Oxford but the course for medicine is much better at Imperial."

"Well, we'll see, dear," said Daphne with a sigh. "We have to sort out your digs first."

"Jeremy went to Christchurch, Oxford," Colin said quietly, anxious to stop his sister from criticising Oxford any further.

"Are you the first in your family to go to university, Sarah?" asked Jeremy archly.

"Yes. Well, no. Mum went to Oxford."

Jeremy was interested now. "Oh, which college?"

"I was at St Hilda's," Daphne replied.

"That's a girls' college."

"Indeed, yes." Daphne smiled sweetly. "No members of the Bullingdon Club at St Hilda's."

The conversation was interrupted by the sound of loud giggles and chatter coming from the downstairs entrance. A moment later, two willowy blonde girls burst into the mess room. Long hair and scarves seemed to be everywhere. Johnny's elder twin sisters had arrived just in time for lunch. There were kisses on both cheeks for Johnny and then for Colin, who had met Miranda and Georgina a few times in London and then on a skiing holiday in Zermatt after his tour in Northern Ireland.

Johnny made the introductions. When it came to Sarah's turn, Miranda kissed her on both cheeks and exclaimed. "So you're Colin's sister and just as gorgeous, darling!" Sarah's face turned crimson.

The last guest for lunch was Jeremy's brother, Robert Kershaw, who had travelled across London from the city where he worked for a firm of solicitors. He was a tall, thin man who looked a little tired after a morning in the city. He was dressed in a well-cut suit but, unlike his brother, his overall appearance was simple; a white shirt, a pale blue tie and buttons on his cuffs rather than expensive cufflinks.

Lunch was a success, much to Colin's relief. His mother sat next to Jeremy, and they chatted comfortably with each other. Colin was happy to have Miranda on one side and his sister Sarah on the other. It gave Colin the chance to catch up on her plans for university later in the year. Johnny was seated on Sarah's other side, and they also seemed to be enjoying themselves.

Robert Kershaw said little during lunch, and Colin wondered if he was anxious about a deal waiting for him in the city later that afternoon. However, during a lull in the conversation, Robert turned towards his brother.

"Jeremy, this is a delicious wine. What is it?" Robert asked.

"I'm glad you like it, Robert," Jeremy replied. "Colin, you picked the wines. Enlighten us if you please?"

"It's a Becker from the Kaiser Stuhl," Colin replied.

"An unusual choice. What made you choose a German wine?" asked Robert.

"I worked there in the summer holidays before I joined the Army."

"Well, you know how to select a good wine," said Robert. "You must come to one of my wine-tasting evenings if my brother can give you some time off. Now I'm afraid I must get back to the city."

After this, lunch soon broke up, and the guests expressed their gratitude and bid farewell. Just before descending the steep flight of stairs to the exit, Daphne Smith reached into her handbag and handed Colin a letter.

"This arrived for you yesterday, Belfast postmark. Look after yourself, darling, and see you soon."

Chapter Nine

While Colin was discussing the wine with his friends and family in St James' Palace, a very different lunchtime gathering was taking place in West Tyrone, Northern Ireland.

The meeting took place at the Smugglers Bar in Clady, very close to Eire's border. This was a safe place for the IRA to meet, as the border was only a short distance away at the halfway point across the bridge over the River Finn. As a show of strength, the IRA had been known to set up checkpoints on Clady Bridge dressed in black berets and dark glasses to mask their identity. This blatant show of strength was made with the sure knowledge that the IRA could slip across the border in seconds if the security forces turned up unexpectedly. In practice, it was very difficult for the British Army to surprise the locals in Clady, who had well-rehearsed early warning systems in place to alert the IRA that a British patrol was approaching.

Only a day before the meeting, Mick the publican, himself a Republican sympathiser, had been told to keep a room free at the back of the bar. He was a big man with a vast beer belly, so big that when he stood at the narrow entrance to his bar, he could prevent unwanted visitors from entering. He wore a sweatshirt that smelled of cheap beer, which was too small for his gut that protruded from the gap between his shirt and the top of his trousers. Standing in the doorway to the Smugglers Bar, he exuded intentional hostility. Only hard-line Republicans were tolerated in his bar, and this made it the perfect venue for a secret meeting.

There were four members of the IRA present at the meeting, and they all arrived separately and by different routes. The first to arrive was Ciaran, a senior member of the Belfast Brigade. He had travelled to Clady by taking the long route around by leaving Northern Ireland, south of Newry, and travelling through Ireland via Castlefinn. Next to arrive was Chloe, who had been hiding in the South since taking part in the RVH shooting attack, where her friend Saraid had been shot dead. She entered the North via Lifford and then Strabane through the border crossing that the Brits called the Hump VCP. The last two to attend were the Flynn brothers, Brendan and Pat. Strabane was their hometown where they lived on the Ballycolman Estate with their mother. Pat had recovered sufficiently from his injuries to move around the town unaided. Meanwhile, Brendan was in fighting form. Only a week before the meeting, he had led an ambush on a British Land Rover patrol near the bridge crossing the River Mourne. One British soldier had been killed, and all the IRA gunmen had escaped without injuries. The IRA council was pleased, and it restored Brendan's reputation with the leadership after the bungled shooting attack in Colinward Street.

Mick escorted each new arrival to the back room without delay. There were only a few regular patrons of the inn present, and these looked straight into their glasses of cheap ale, avoiding eye contact with the newcomers. When all four were present, Ciaran immediately took charge of the meeting.

"We had a council meeting last week. I'm not going to give you the details, but we're concerned. The Brits have their bloody spies everywhere, and it's difficult for us to attack without the RUC or the fucking Brits knowing in advance." Ciaran paused and looked around the room. No one looked happy. He decided to continue, "Our last two attacks in Belfast were a failure—"

"I still shot a Brit," Brendan interrupted. "Nobody in the Belfast Brigade was up for the job."

"Yeah, but no one was killed; we wanted at least two dead Brits. They also shot Pat. Then there was that mess in the RVH."

"That was not my fault! Saraid should have shot that Brit before he shot her."

"Don't speak ill of the dead!" Chloe now entered the conversation and looked at Brendan accusingly. "You didn't mind screwing her right up to her death. She was a good friend to me, and I want to shoot the bloody Brit that killed her!"

"The papers say he was the same Brit who rescued our sister Mary in the Ardoyne," said Pat quietly.

"He's still a fucking Brit!" said Brendan.

"OK, calm down; let's calm down," said Ciaran. "Listen to what we plan to do, and maybe some of you will get what you want. We're going to attack the Brits in the UK. Anything we do there gets much more attention. We've got to do something to make the Brits withdraw totally from Ireland. We've got a plan and we've brought in an outsider to do the job."

"You mean a bloody mercenary!" Brendan's voice was loud and angry.

"Look, we've got to. He's not known to any of our volunteers, so he can move freely. He's OK. Jerry has met him."

"Who is he?" Pat asked.

"Look, shut up. Jerry wants this done! For now, you don't need to know." The two mentions of Jerry restored some order to the meeting.

"Brendan and Chloe, you're going to London. Your job will be to provide backup when needed."

"What the fuck am I going to do in London?" shouted Brendan.

"You get a job that gives you a reason to drive around and somewhere to stay. Our boys in Kilburn will help you out. You've got the perfect cover; you can say you want to see more of your sister, who's starting as a student."

"I don't like Mary being in bloody London. She should stay here in Ireland with her ma."

"It works for us, her being in London," Ciaran persisted. "And she doesn't need to know what you're doing."

"So far, I don't know what I'm bloody doing."

The discussion was getting very heated and bad-tempered. They were also too noisy, and Ciaran was getting concerned about security. He wanted to wrap up the meeting quickly but without appearing weak.

He was saved by Mick, the publican.

"A British patrol has just left their base in Sion Mills and is heading this way."

Although, so far as they knew, none of the group were actually on the run, they were all known as Provo supporters. For the four of them to be seen meeting together would be a major error. As a result, the meeting broke up quickly and they all left the bar and headed off in different directions. Ciaran as the most senior took the short trip across the border on Clady Bridge. He would then have a long trip back to Belfast, re-entering Northern Ireland near Dundalk. Chloe had a car outside the bar, and a volunteer was waiting to drive her into Strabane to stay in a safe house in the Townsend Estate for a few days before driving back to Eire. Brendan and Pat were the last to leave. As local boys, it would not raise suspicion for them to be seen drinking in the Smugglers Bar, something they did occasionally anyway. They went and stood by the bar, where there were now four other drinkers.

One of these drinkers was Martin Ewing, an unemployed man on benefits with a wife and three children living on the Ballycolman Estate in Strabane. Martin did odd jobs for cash in Castlefinn over the border in Eire, where he also had a mistress, and liked to break his journey at the Smugglers Bar on his way back to his family in Strabane. Martin nodded a greeting to Brendan and Pat when they bought drinks at the bar, but he avoided starting a conversation. Brendan Flynn was feared in and around Strabane. After finishing his beer, Martin murmured a brief farewell to Mick and shuffled out of the bar.

Martin walked south for two hundred metres and found his car parked on the side of the road. He didn't like to park too close to the bar, making it more difficult for anyone to tell exactly what time he arrived and left. He unlocked the car and climbed inside. He need not have bothered locking his car, which was a wreck held together by rust, and hadn't passed a MOT for over a year. Martin just hoped the car would get him home safely without being stopped by the RUC. Fortunately for Martin, the RUC rarely patrolled this part of West Tyrone and even when they did, they needed half a platoon of British infantry in support.

As a result, less than half an hour later, without any trouble, Martin parked his car outside his home on Ballycolman Drive. Before going inside, he checked that the sun visors were down on both the driver's and front passenger's side. He also put a small road atlas of Northern Ireland on the dashboard.

Chapter Ten

Once Mary Flynn had finished her shopping in Strabane's town centre she headed south towards the River Foyle. There wasn't very much in her small shopping bag, and there hadn't been much to choose from in any case. Strabane had the highest number of unemployed people in Europe, and there was little money changing hands in its shops.

To be honest, the main reason for her shopping trip was to get out of the house on Ballycolman Drive. There had been a tearful but happy reunion with her mother when Mary arrived back in Strabane. She had been discharged from the RVH a few days after the shooting and, after a brief visit to her shared house in Ardoyne, she took the long bus journey to her home town. Her mother had been so happy and relieved to see her and for a week or so, they were relaxed in each other's company.

Mary turned onto Bridge Street and approached the Brit checkpoint on the north side of the bridge, which crossed the River Foyle. She walked between the two ugly concrete sangars that straddled the north side of the bridge. Two British soldiers were checking cars and pedestrians and more Brits stared down at her from inside the sangars. Mary felt she was being eyed up and wished she was wearing a longer skirt to cover her legs. She knew she had good legs and liked to show them off, but not in front of the Brits. The officer on duty told her to open her bag to check the contents, only to find her meagre purchases. He was quite good-looking, but not as handsome as the Brit she had met in the RVH. Mary wondered what he was doing now. From the papers, she learned that his name was Colin Smith, and he was probably now chatting up the English girls in London. Mary's mother, Colleen, had been very upset to hear that her only daughter was going to London. Colleen had never left Ireland, and apart from an occasional trip to Derry, she rarely ventured beyond Strabane. The thought that her daughter, always top of her class at St Colman's, was going to be so far away and surrounded by Brits was hard for her to understand.

Mary reached the southern bank of the river and turned south-east towards the Ballycolman Estate. She wondered if her two brothers would be at home. Brendan and Pat were both angry, while her mother had been both upset and proud of her daughter as she planned to move to London. Brendan was particularly annoyed at the thought of Mary 'moving' in with the Brits.

Mary had always had a difficult relationship with her elder brothers. Pat, who was two years older, was fundamentally a gentle soul but lived his life in Brendan's shadow. Brendan, on the other hand, was six years older than Mary and he took his role as the eldest of the three very seriously, particularly after their father died while serving a sentence for the attempted murder of an off-duty RUC constable. Brendan had a very hot temper and held very pro-republican views. Mary was certain that both her brothers were in the IRA but did not know any details, and past questions on the subject had provoked an angry response from Brendan. Brendan had offered no explanation for his presence in Belfast after the Ardoyne bombing. Furthermore, she had been given no details about poor Pat's wounding.

Mary turned up on Ballycolman Avenue and did up her short coat. It started to rain, and it was damp near the river. Mary asked herself yet again what her two brothers did all day. After her siblings' initial hostile reaction to her plans to study in London, she was astonished this morning when Brendan announced that not only should Mary go to London, but that he was planning to do the same! He needed to get a job, he said. *Well, we certainly need the money*, thought Mary. Both Brendan and Pat were on benefits and Mary's low earnings as a nurse would soon cease when she went to London.

Mary sighed as she approached their home in Ballycolman Drive, not looking forward to consoling her mother. She noticed Martin Ewing's car parked on the other side of the street with both sun visors down, but there had been little sun recently. Mary wondered how Martin's car was still drivable and would surely not pass its MOT. But then no one from the RUC would glance at Martin's car so long as it was parked in the Ballycolman Estate, where the police feared to tread.

Mary didn't notice the young couple in a car driving along the other side of the road.

Chapter Eleven

Major Smith was not really Major Smith at all. His real name was Grenville – not that many people were aware of the fact. But he preferred to be called Smith. He wasn't a major either; in fact, he wasn't even in the Army, but it suited him to have a rank when surrounded by so many staff officers at Headquarters Northern Ireland. As a senior member of MI5, and with service in the past with the Secret Intelligence Service, he was equivalent to at least a lieutenant general in rank but plain Major suited Grenville better and with his greying hair, he could pass easily for an ageing major in danger of being passed over.

He had intense discussions with Commander Land Forces and the Army's intelligence staff immediately after the shooting attack in the RVH. Up until then, Grenville was fairly happy with the way the intelligence war was proceeding. The Security Services, which included the RUC's Special Branch, had infiltrated the IRA leadership in Belfast so that Grenville and his team knew more or less when and where the IRA would attack. However, the IRA responded by bringing in outsiders, and Grenville's network was not as strong outside Belfast as it was within the city. The Colinward shooting was the first IRA attack about which Grenville had had no inkling for a long time.

Then shortly afterwards, there was that chaotic shooting at the RVH, where, again, there had been no warning.

Grenville responded by posing as a member of the military police when they went to interview that cocky young Guards Officer, Colin Smith. He then put more effort into exploiting his assets outside Belfast, which appeared to be what the IRA was also doing.

When two intelligence officers from the Det made their weekly drive through the Ballycolman Estate in Strabane, passing Martin Ewing's parked-up wreck of a car, they noted that both sun visors were down. Both sun visors down meant Martin had something to report but the road atlas on the dashboard meant that he wanted an urgent meeting the next day. Grenville ran a safe house in Ballymagorry, just outside Strabane, a small village where most people were retired and lived quietly. Martin could claim to anyone who asked that he had some building work in the village. This work was provided by Grenville and consisted of some minor repairs to the bathroom in the safe house. The evening before the meeting, Grenville moved into the property. He arrived in a car, wearing a suit and carrying a small overnight case. He made sure his duty-free bag was visible to any neighbours who might be watching. He looked like a businessman returning home from an overseas trip. While it was still light, Grenville pottered in the garden and dug up some of the weeds that had grown while he had been away. He put the weeds in a small wheelbarrow, which he then emptied onto a compost heap at the end of the garden. When he had finished, he returned the wheelbarrow to the front of the house and left a garden rake by its side.

The next morning, Grenville woke up early, made himself a cup of coffee and took a brief stroll in the garden. He checked that the garden rake was still leaning against the wheelbarrow, signalling that it was safe for Martin Ewing to enter the property. Grenville hoped he would arrive at nine a.m., as agreed.

Martin arrived five minutes late. *Not too bad,* thought Grenville but he said nothing. Both Martin and Grenville spent five minutes in the bathroom initially so that Martin could describe the work he was doing if someone asked him later.

When they were finished in the bathroom, they went to a small bedroom at the back of the house, where no one could see them from the quiet estate outside.

Grenville was keen to take control and start the meeting as quickly as possible. "Were you followed?" he asked. This was just to assert his authority; he knew Martin hadn't been followed because, if he had, the members of the detachment who were staking out the safe house would have warned him.

"Don't think so," Martin replied. "Anyway, I'm just on a building job, aren't I?"

Grenville doubted whether Martin could have spotted any sort of tail. "Why did you make the signal for an emergency meeting?" he asked.

"Was drinking at the Smugglers two nights ago," said Martin.

Grenville suppressed a sigh. "You drink there most nights, Martin. What about it?"

"There was a meeting in the back room."

"Go on," said Grenville.

"It was all hush-hush. Even fat Mick was jumpy and nervous. I just drank my beer and minded my own business."

"Who was at the meeting? Did you see anything?"

"Yeah. The two Flynn boys, Brendan and Pat. Brendan's an evil bastard…"

"Who else?"

"Don't know; it's not local though."

"How do you know? I thought you said you were just minding your business." Grenville was now interested.

"There was a girl with a Belfast accent, all dressed up like a tart."

"So you spoke to them?"

"No! Of course I fucking didn't! However, there was shouting. We could hear them in the bar."

"What did you hear?"

"They were talking about London. One of them said, 'I don't want to go to bloody London'!"

Chapter Twelve

Royal Victoria Hospital
Falls Road
Belfast
Dear Colin,
I hope you don't mind me calling you Colin. I'm not very good at ranks and titles, except for the medical world, I suppose. I hope that by the time you get this, you are nearly healed.

That was a black day, Colin. We've never had a shooting inside the hospital, only a few times in the grounds. You were in a bad way after you shot Saraid. I wanted to nurse you, but the Brits rushed you away so fast that I didn't get the chance. Sorry, I know you are a Brit as well.

What a lot of questions from the bloody RUC! I've never liked them since I was a girl growing up in the Markets. They wanted to know what I saw – which was precious little – and who everyone was. Of course, I knew Saraid from when she was a nurse at the Royal; she was a tough girl and didn't like being told what to do. I wasn't sorry when she left but I didn't know she'd joined the Provos, though I shouldn't be surprised.

I miss dear Mary a lot. She was such a sweet girl and one of my best nurses. She left us as soon as she got better, saying she wanted to be a doctor and train in London of all places! I'm afraid I don't have an address for her but if she gets in touch, I can tell her you were asking after her. Her family is from Strabane, which is a tough town so it is!

A few days after the shooting, a couple of the boys came to visit me at home. I think they thought they could frighten me, but I told them I'd grown up with much tougher people in the Markets. They asked me the same questions that the RUC had asked, and I told them I knew nothing, which is pretty much the truth.

They were interested in you, Colin. Be very careful if you ever come back to Belfast.

I hope you're staying well and God bless you.

Yours,
Kath.

Colin read Sister Kath's letter yet again. When he had finished, he put the letter carefully in his desk drawer and started to get ready for the evening ahead.

He had read the same words many times since his mother handed him the letter on leaving Queen's Guard nearly two months ago. Every time the letter brought him back to West Belfast. Colin found this disquieting, as it distracted him from his busy and enjoyable life as a Guards officer in London.

At first, Colin greatly enjoyed the hectic merry-go-round of drinks, parties, trips to the cinema, Ascot and more guard duties at both St James' Palace and the Tower of London. The summer had passed in a blur but now as autumn approached, the excitement of public duties was beginning to fade.

His best friend, Johnny Keynsham, had been sent on the Platoon Commanders Course in Warminster, and Colin missed him. Johnny's twin sisters, Miranda and Georgina, had recently embarked on a long trip to Australia and their father, the Earl of Cheltenham, was only too glad to let his Australian cousins take charge of his troublesome daughters for a while. Colin missed them as well, particularly Miranda with whom Colin had a brief relationship that started in Zermatt and continued over the summer. But they had ceased to be lovers for over a month now as Miranda's trip to Australia drew closer and her attention wandered.

To make matters worse, Colin did not like Johnny Keynsham's replacement, Iain Munro, who was a little older than Colin and had been commissioned a few intakes before him. Munro liked to mock Colin about his background, even calling him the grammar school boy to his face. Initially, Colin had to accept this verbal bullying, as newly commissioned officers were not expected even to speak to their fellow officers for the first few months in the Officers' Mess. Fortunately, Munro was posted to the Windsor Battalion just before the Belfast tour, and he didn't see Munro again until Johnny's ski holiday in

Zermatt while the Battalion was on post-tour leave. Munro had been a bore throughout the holiday, particularly with the girls who didn't like even sharing a chair lift with him. But now he was back and had just been made Assistant Adjutant, and he relished dishing out extra picket duties to punish his junior officers, and Colin in particular, for minor offences.

Colin put on his suit jacket and checked his tie. He was going to spend the evening with his sister in Kilburn. It seemed absurd to be wearing a suit to go and spend an evening with Sarah and her student friends, but the rules for Guards officers were very strict and a suit had to be worn when walking past the barrack guard and through the front gate onto Lower Sloane Street. After leaving Chelsea Barracks, Colin turned right and headed to Sloane Square, where he was going to risk taking the tube. This was totally out of order for Guards officers who were not allowed to use public transport except for black taxis. Colin hoped he wouldn't be spotted and reported to Munro.

After changing at Victoria, Colin was glad to arrive at Kilburn Tube, where he took off his tie and slung his suit jacket over his shoulder. It was a short walk to Galton Street, and he wound his way through a maze of short streets with terraced housing on both sides of the road. Colin thought that most houses needed repair and one house with a large skip blocking the pavement to its front had been gutted. The builders had finished for the day, leaving the house as an empty shell. Colin turned left into Third Avenue, passing the White Swan which was doing good business. Music that could have been folk songs and loud Irish accents came from within. It reminded Colin of Murphy's Bar on Springfield Road.

Shortly after, Colin arrived at 14 Galton Street. This was another terraced house in need of repair, like most of the other properties nearby. Sarah shared the house with three other first-year medical students who, between them, could just afford the rent. There was enough noise to rival the White Swan in the next street and Sarah's party was evidently in full swing. The front door was not locked, and Colin managed to squeeze himself into the tiny hallway at the foot of a steep flight of stairs, on which student couples were sitting and talking and laughing loudly. Sarah let him leave a pair of jeans in her room on the first floor, which was crammed with people, so Colin waited outside the tiny bathroom next to her room to change. Eventually, a young couple emerged from the bathroom, barely noticing Colin before re-joining the party.

Colin went to find his sister, meeting young students who he had met over the past few weeks. He had enjoyed his recent trips to see his sister. It made a welcome change from the stuffiness of Chelsea Barracks. On the landing, there was a gramophone that had seen better days playing Abba's Dancing Queen at full volume. Colin edged past the gramophone, taking care not to knock it, and saw Sarah in her flatmate's bedroom talking to a girl with blonde hair; her back was towards him, and Colin wondered if they had met before. Then, the couple who had been together in the bathroom earlier collided with the gramophone and the music stopped abruptly. There was a collective groan, and everyone turned towards the landing.

And there she was.

Mary and Colin made eye contact immediately. Her hair had grown a little, and she seemed to have fully recovered from her injuries. They were both very surprised to see each other again, and Colin walked over to her to say something. But he did not know what to say, and they looked at each other a little shyly. They were saved by the music; the gramophone had been restored, and Abba was now singing their song SOS. It was difficult to hear anything, and Sarah shouted something about Mary being on the same course at Imperial. Everyone was dancing; bottles of cheap wine were everywhere, and Colin thought he smelt marijuana. Colin and Mary started to dance, a little apart at first, but their bodies soon touched and drew closer and closer to each other for the rest of the night.

From his battered van on the other side of Galton Street, Brendan Flynn watched the party.

Chapter Thirteen

"I hate bloody London!" said Brendan Flynn loudly. He was alone in his builder's van, so there was little chance of anyone hearing; not that anyone would care about his opinion in any case. He hated the smug English and their ways of patronising and laughing at the Irish; his blood boiled when he heard how the struggle for freedom in Ireland was reported in the press and he longed to be back on his side of the water.

But his orders were very clear; get somewhere to stay, get a job and get a van. He had been told to ask for Martin in O'Neill's, a pub off the Kilburn High Road, who fixed him up with a small room in a hostel nearby. Martin also arranged for him to work as a driver for a small firm of builders, ferrying equipment from site to site across North London. His pay was low, but he had the use of the van twenty-four hours a day. He had been told he should see his sister occasionally; supporting his cover of both someone needing work in London and keeping an eye on his young sister at the same time. Of course, he could say nothing about his real purpose in London.

The truth was that much of the time Brendan Flynn was bored. He rang the number he had been given once a week from the call box at the back of O'Neill's but to date, he had been told to do nothing except wait, be patient, and keep out of trouble. But Flynn was not good at being patient and he was even worse at staying out of trouble; spending too much time at O'Neill's had not been good for Brendan. At first, the pub seemed like the obvious sanctuary for Brendan; most of the customers had Irish roots, and everyone enjoyed singing Republican songs, which grew louder and louder up till closing time. But Brendan soon became frustrated and, after a short while, his fellow drinkers began to irritate him. They were good enough at singing songs about the fight for Irish freedom, but none of them had the bottle to do anything useful other than drink, talk and sing.

Brendan decided to end his vigil over his sister and return to his digs. He was not supposed to see too much of his sister in any case.

The next morning, he rose early and went to meet Chloe at a small café in West Kensington, as agreed.

"You look all dressed up," said Brendan, sliding onto a bench opposite Chloe.

Chloe wasn't sure whether to take this as a compliment or not. "We're going to bloody South Kensington and we were told to blend in," Chloe replied.

Brendan grunted and picked up a greasy menu. "I fancy a full Irish."

"You mean full English! And keep your voice down," Chloe hissed. She had found working with Brendan a strain; he had such a quick temper and always seemed to look angry. He had not made much effort to smarten himself up for the visit to South Kensington, and Chloe realised she would have to explain him as a paid help if anyone asked questions. She waited until he had finished his breakfast, wiping his mouth with his sleeve, before running through the plan for the day. Brendan was supposed to drive to Heathrow in his builder's van and park in the long-stay car park. Then he would collect a blue Ford Cortina that would be parked nearby and drive it to Ovington Gardens; he was not to open the boot nor linger at Heathrow. Chloe made sure that Brendan had memorised the registration of the Cortina and the address in Ovington Gardens.

After leaving the café, Brendan and Chloe went their separate ways. Chloe took the tube, exited the Piccadilly line at Knightsbridge underground station and walked south west along Brompton Road, passing Harrods and other shops on the way; everything looked so affluent compared to any city centre in Ireland. After passing Beauchamp Place, she turned left into Ovington Gardens, looking out for 32A, a small house that was sandwiched between two large mansion blocks that appeared to have been converted into flats. Chloe reached into her pocket for her keys and approached the front door. She kept repeating her cover story in her head.

"I'm doing a favour for a friend I met on holiday; he's still abroad but needs someone to open up his house. I only met him once, in a bar in Dublin, and he gave me twenty quid to open his house. He's anticipating the delivery of some fancy crockery. No, I only know his first name, Simon."

As it happened, Chloe entered the house without anyone showing any interest, and all she had to do now was wait for Brendan in his Ford Cortina. Chloe thought of looking around the house but remembered her briefing; don't be nosy and don't touch anything! Fortunately, Chloe did not have long to wait, and the doorbell rang shortly after she arrived at the house. Brendan had managed to park the Cortina immediately in front of the front door. "Delivery for 32A Ovington Gardens, madam." Chloe hoped he was not overplaying his part and watched him return to the car, open the boot and start to unload the contents: brightly wrapped boxes and parcels, even two large hat boxes decorated professionally with a bright ribbon. An onlooker would have observed the delivery of a very expensive shopping expedition, perhaps before a birthday party. Once the goods were safely delivered, Brendan drove away in the Cortina and parked the vehicle in Lexham Gardens as previously instructed before taking the bus back to Heathrow to retrieve his builder's van.

Chloe waited in Ovington Gardens for forty-five minutes, resisting the temptation to open the parcels or look around the house, so she sat on a hard-backed chair and stared at the wall for a bit, then checked her good looks in a mirror that was the only wall covering in the hall apart from a print of a loch that reminded her of a summer spent on school camp in Co Fermanagh a few years ago.

When Chloe left the house, she locked up and posted the keys back through the letterbox. Once her visit was over, she was told to forget about Ovington Gardens, which now stood empty until the arrival of its mysterious owner.

Chapter Fourteen

The IRA's top agent in the British Army was a young Guards officer called Iain Munro.

To all appearances, Iain Munro had the perfect background for a career in the Guards. Educated at Radley and then Bristol University, he was commissioned via an Army university cadetship that was difficult to obtain. The three years spent at Bristol counted as years of service, so when he arrived in his battalion, he was senior to several of his brother officers who had joined the Army directly from school.

He was one of the Munro family who had been in Scotland for generations, acquiring land over the centuries through a combination of greed, violence and intimidation. By the 1970s, the family owned large estates in Perthshire and Aberdeenshire, and the head of the family, Murray Munro, the Earl of Cairnie, had his seat at Cairnie Castle just east of Perth from where he managed his estates, shot grouse in the late summer and fished in the River Tay. Unlike his violent ancestors, Murray Munro was a kindly soul and a benign landowner who liked to take care that his tenants were properly looked after. Murray Munro had never married and had inherited the title and the Cairnie estates from his elder brother, who had been killed in the

Second World War, also without issue. As a result, the heir presumptive to the Earldom and the estates was Murray's distant cousin, young Iain Munro, a newly commissioned officer in the British Army who came from the Irish side of the family.

While downplaying his Irish roots, Iain Munro took great care in promoting his Scottish background and the fact that one day he would be the Earl of Cairnie. He made sure that he invited the right friends to shoot and fish in Scotland; these would be the likes of Johnny Keynsham, whose family also owned an estate in Gloucestershire, and more senior officers, like Jeremy Kershaw, who could help him with his career. He made sure that he never invited Colin, who assumed that his grammar school background precluded him from ever joining Munro's select gatherings.

But there was a much darker reason why Munro never invited Colin to his uncle's estates in Perthshire. Colin was sharp and asked awkward questions about Ireland.

While the Munro clan was acquiring land in Scotland, some members of the family saw similar opportunities in Ireland and established themselves there with a ruthlessness similar to that of their Scottish cousins. Over the centuries, the Irish side of the family added the letter 'E' to the end of their surnames, becoming the Munroe family.

By the early 1950s, the Munroes in Ireland had developed into a family of commerce. Gone were the country estates which had been replaced by a chain of pubs, betting shops, garages and commercial property on both sides of the border between Northern Ireland and Ireland. From an office in the Waterside district of Londonderry, Robert Munroe, the head of the Irish side of the family, managed this successful chain of enterprises that he had inherited from his father at the end of the Second World War.

Two weeks before Christmas in 1951, Robert Munroe hosted the firm's annual party at Ryan's Inn, one of the pubs the family owned in Strabane. It was there that he met Chrissie Maguire, one of the pretty young barmaids who worked at Ryan's Inn behind the bar. The pubs had done well that year, and Robert had offered a night of free drinks for all the staff as a reward for all their hard work over the past twelve months. Needless to say, everyone at the party was very soon inebriated. Chrissie enjoyed herself so much that she soon started to flirt with her boss. Robert had not intended to drink very much, but the pretty young Chrissie encouraged him to have just one drink, and then another, and then one or two more.

The next morning, Robert woke up in the back seat of his car in the pub's car park. The first thing he knew was that he had a dreadful hangover, then secondly, that he was nearly naked, and thirdly, that Chrissie, also wearing little, was asleep beside him in his car. Robert nudged and prodded Chrissie until she groaned, and then realised where she was and what may have happened. There was a frantic search for clothing until Chrissie staggered out of the car and back towards the pub to join the others in clearing up after the party. Meanwhile, Robert, nursing his hangover, drove back to the family's office in Londonderry to start a day's work.

In the weeks that followed, Robert continued to run the family business, and the events of the Christmas party began to blur in his memory. That was until one morning, when his secretary informed him that a young girl was asking for him at reception, and Robert knew even before seeing Chrissie, looking pale and anxious, that his troubles were about to begin.

Chrissie was due to have a baby in six months' time, and she insisted that the father could only be Robert. If this was not difficult enough, there were other major problems. Robert's family was Protestant, and his family was firmly embedded in the Unionist community of Northern Ireland. Robert's mother, who was still alive, was also a pillar of the church in the Waterside. Eileen Munroe had long wanted Robert to settle down and start a family, especially since the death of Robert's father. Eileen had engineered several supper parties and other social gatherings where Robert could meet a nice girl from the right sort of family.

But Eileen Munroe did not regard Chrissie's family as the right sort at all. The Maguires were a poor working-class family who lived in little more than a slum dwelling on the edge of Strabane, while the Munroes were one of the wealthiest families in Northern Ireland. But the biggest problem, by far, was that the Maguires were Roman Catholics and a part of Strabane's local religious community. To make matters even worse, the Maguires had strong links to Irish nationalism, and Chrissie's father had even fought with Michael Collins in the aftermath of the Easter Uprising in 1916.

And yet, despite these difficulties, Robert Munroe and Chrissie Maguire were married on a spring day in 1952. The impending arrival of Chrissie's baby had forced both families to compromise, and the prospect of a child born out of wedlock was as bad as a mixed marriage. A church on neutral ground was found in Limavady, with both a Church of Ireland and a Roman Catholic priest presiding, followed by a short honeymoon in Scotland. Then, in September, Ian Munroe was born to a delighted mother and father in Derry.

As Ian grew up, he divided his time between his home in Derry and Chrissie's family in Strabane. Chrissie's parents were not well, and a lifetime spent in poorly heated housing with little money had taken its toll. However, Chrissie's brother, Ciaran Maguire, was full of life. While Chrissie was pretty, Ciaran had not inherited any good looks from his parents and, with a curiously shaped mouth and jaw, he looked very much like a rat. He was also an ardent Republican, and he was very proud of his father, who had worked in intelligence with Michael Collins in the early days of the Irish Civil War. Ciaran took an interest in his nephew Ian, and as soon as he was old enough, enjoyed telling him stories about the Irish fight for freedom and independence from the evil British state.

Robert Munroe would have chosen to reduce the time his son spent with his brother-in-law, Ciaran, but he was forever busy running his business, and Chrissie was happy to be with her side of the family while Robert was hard at work. Then, just after Ian's eighth birthday, a tragic event occurred that shaped Ian's life forever. Eileen Maguire had to have some medical tests at the newly opened Altnagelvin Hospital and, in case she was not safe to drive, Robert said he would collect his mother and drive her home. As they both walked to Robert's car, Eileen explained to her son that the tests had not discovered anything serious and that she was in fine health for her age. They were both so busy talking that they paid little attention to the traffic and never saw the red Cortina driving well over the speed limit in the hospital car park. They were both hit and thrown sideways by the force of the car; a couple of nurses going off duty immediately came to their aid, and they were rushed inside to intensive care, but they were pronounced dead shortly after. The red Cortina, which turned out to be stolen, never stopped and was later found abandoned on the Strabane Old Road.

Chapter Fifteen

Ian Munroe had just started at Sunny Meadows Preparatory School for Boys at the time of his father's tragic death. The school was in Cheshire and there was little that was sunny about it. It seemed to Ian that it rained even more in Cheshire than he was used to in Northern Ireland. It was almost a relief to go to his father's funeral so that he could escape from the school for a few days, and Ian longed to go to a day school in Northern Ireland. It was Robert Munroe who had insisted that his son should go to a school in England, and Chrissie would have readily moved her son's schooling back to Northern Ireland after her husband's death. But curiously, her brother Ciaran persuaded her to keep Ian at Sunny Meadows because his prospects would be better at an English school. The death of Robert Munroe also prompted a sudden interest in Ian from Mungo Munro in Scotland; Ian was now heir to the Scottish estates, and Mungo also preferred traditional schooling for his young cousin.

Ian loathed Sunny Meadows. He was bullied mercilessly by the other boys, who made fun of his Irish accent and called him a variety of cruel names. For the first year, his life at school was miserable; when the taunts of being called 'bog Irish' or a 'Fenian bastard' grew too much, he was sometimes reduced to tears, encouraging his tormentors to be even nastier. Ian often thought of running away, but with no money, the prospect of reaching Liverpool and stowing away on a ferry to Ireland was too much.

The school was badly run. The Headmaster, Major Wright, had served in the Royal Marines during World War II, apparently with distinction. Unfortunately, his bravery on the battlefield did not extend to running a good boarding school; beatings were common, bullying was ignored and the teaching was poor; only one master had been to university and he had to leave after an incident with a member of the choir in the squash court. The school's administration was equally bad, especially after the Bursar's rapid departure at the start of the Lent term, along with the savings for the First XV's rugby tour to Ireland planned for the Easter holidays.

One consequence of the school's incompetence was that the boys' records were frequently muddled and misfiled, so one boy's details were sometimes confused with another. There was a boy in his final year at the school whose name was also Iain Munro, but spelt with an extra letter 'I' in Iain and without an e at the end of the surname. Ian's name was increasingly spelt the same way on school lists and even on end-of-term reports.

At long last, Ian's first year at Sunny Meadows came to an end and it was time for the long summer holidays. The plan was for Ian, or Iain, as he let people call him, to spend half the holidays with Mungo Munro in Scotland

and the other half in Strabane. At first, Iain found his time in Perthshire rather intimidating, but he soon enjoyed the vast estate surrounding Cairnie Castle and the variety of activities on offer. He also found his cousin Mungo a bit frightening at first, but they gradually warmed to each other, and, after a while, he addressed him as his Uncle Mungo. Mungo encouraged him when it came to field sports – fishing in the River Tay – and, after the 12th of August, he even had a brief attempt at shooting grouse at one of Mungo's expensive shoots. When it was time to leave Scotland to return to his mother and his uncle in Northern Ireland, Iain was surprised to find that he was sorry to leave Scotland.

Following the death of her husband, Chrissie still owned the property in the Waterside district of Londonderry but spent more and more of her time in Strabane with her brother Ciaran. Her late husband had left her very comfortably off financially, with a trust fund to secure their son's future. The Munroe businesses continued to be run by a board of trustees, with young Ian being the majority shareholder.

Iain Munro was shocked to see his mother when he returned to Derry. She had gained weight; her skin was damp when he gave her a dutiful kiss on the cheek; and her hair was lank and greasy. If Iain had been older, he would probably have realised that his mother had turned into a heavy drinker. She listened to her son's account of boarding school and his recent stay in Scotland, but she appeared distracted and lethargic when talking to her son.

The only time Chrissie brightened up was when they discussed their visit to her brother Ciaran the following day in Strabane.

Ciaran, on the other hand, was taking more and more of a keen interest in Iain's future. He listened intently to his description of Sunny Meadows and wanted to know all the small details, including the misspelling of his surname and the bullying. When he heard that one of the other boys, Rufus Metcalf, enjoyed whipping Iain with a wet towel, Ciaran muttered grimly, "We'll have to do something about that!" Ciaran was also very interested in Iain's stay in Scotland. Despite the very different worlds of Strabane in Northern Ireland and Cairnie Castle in Perthshire, Ciaran supported his nephew's trip to stay with his Scottish cousin and was all ears to the descriptions of those he met as well as the field sports on offer. Over the summer in Strabane, Ciaran kept Iain busy with trips to Loch Erne, where he went hiking and fishing. He also made Iain join a gym run by the Flynn family, where he learnt the basics of boxing. Iain found this difficult at first and felt awkward and shy among the local boys from Strabane, but he soon adapted by reverting to his local accent, which he had suppressed while at Sunny Meadows.

For those masters at Sunny Meadows who took an interest in their pupils, Ian Munroe (or was his name Iain Munro?) returned to the school with a new confidence. He had grown a few inches, and after all the fresh air in the countryside had spread out across his shoulders. The pupils also noticed a change in Iain Munro, and they listened in awe to his stories of fishing and stalking in the highlands of Scotland. Iain never mentioned his stay in Ireland, and he was increasingly thought of as a Scot, finding it easy to speak with an English accent when in England and reverting to his native Irish when in Strabane.

Not all of Iain's schoolmates liked his new confidence, and Rufus Metcalf planned an attack to reassert his dominance. With one of his gang members in support, Rufus planned an ambush in the changing room outside the showers. But Iain knew very well that Rufus planned an attack, and with memories of being whipped with wet towels still fresh in his mind, he guessed that the showers and changing rooms would be the battleground. As a result, he had hidden a cricket stump amongst his games clothes, and he had this wrapped in a towel whenever he went to the showers. Shortly after the start of term, after Colts Football, Iain took a shower, returned to the changing room, and as expected, there was Rufus with one of his gang.

"Fenian bastard!" Rufus began, "You've been getting too big for your boots."

"Just leave me alone to change," Iain replied.

But Rufus took a swipe with the wet towel that just missed Iain's arm. One of Rufus's gang members went behind Iain, who knew that he had to act quickly. Dropping his towel, he revealed the cricket stump and swerving full circle, he caught the boy behind on his kneecap, who howled in pain and fell. Rufus was so astonished that he stood gaping at Iain for a couple of seconds, which was all the time Iain needed to press home his advantage. Using the cricket stump like a fencer's foil, he prodded Rufus sharply several times, with the pointed end forcing Rufus to step backwards.

After a few steps backwards, Rufus slipped and fell against a bench littered with dirty games clothes. Iain was quick to take advantage and rammed the cricket stump widthways, with a hand holding each end under Rufus's chin, forcing him to lie on his back with Iain sitting on his chest, making it nearly impossible for Rufus to breathe. Iain looked around and noticed that his other attacker had fled, possibly to seek help. As a result, Iain released the pressure and let Rufus recover, who was badly shaken but unscarred apart from some redness on his throat.

No member of the school's staff even acknowledged that the incident had ever occurred, but no one ever tried bullying Iain again.

The rest of Iain's schooldays fell into an ordered routine. He grew into a confident and bright schoolboy both in the classroom and on the sports pitch, where he was in the First XV in his final year at Sunny Meadows. In the holidays, he would stay mostly with his cousin Mungo in Scotland, shooting, stalking and fishing, all of which exploits he would boast about loudly back at school. Then, for about a week every holiday, he would slip over to Northern Ireland to see his mother and his uncle Ciaran for various activities about which he said nothing to his schoolmates.

These activities started with talking about Ireland and its long struggle with England. They would speak a great deal about how badly the minority Roman Catholic population were treated in Northern Ireland; the very humble Maguire home, little more than a slum, bore witness to this state of affairs.

When it came to Common Entrance, the Headmaster recommended trying one of the minor public schools in Cheshire or nearby Shropshire that were prepared to take boys from Sunny Meadows who usually performed poorly in the Common Entrance exam. But Mungo Munro, who had been at Radley, insisted that Iain, who now always spelt his name with an 'I', should at least try for his alma mater.

Of course, the Headmaster of Sunny Meadows strongly advised against Iain trying for Radley; no one from the school had passed into any major public school for nearly ten years, and the masters were ill-equipped to prepare Iain properly. But Mungo Munro insisted and even offered to pay for extra tuition – an offer the school readily accepted, with the school's finances in a parlous state. Ciaran was also keen for Iain to go to Radley for various reasons, and he made sure Chrissie supported Mungo's plan.

When Iain passed his common entrance for Radley, the masters at Sunny Meadows were so astonished that the Headmaster announced an extra school holiday.

Radley worked perfectly for Iain and Ciaran's plan. No one else from Sunny Meadows made it to the school and so Iain was able to portray himself as he wanted. He never mentioned his mother in Northern Ireland and gave the impression that his closest relative was his Uncle Mungo in Perthshire.

Ever since hurting Rufus Metcalf outside the showers at Sunny Meadows, Iain found that he developed a taste for violence and inflicting pain on others. Over the next five years at public school, there were several opportunities, and Iain particularly enjoyed the planning of these attacks. He would decide on his target – another boy he did not like, or even a master, especially if someone had mocked the Irish – and then work out when and where his ambush would take place. Ciaran had warned him that he must not arouse the suspicion of others; it was vital that he continued to be regarded as the model public school boy. But Iain found that the requirements of secrecy and anonymity made the attacks all the more thrilling. He started modestly and simply, sometimes not even laying a hand on his victim. There was a broom cupboard a few doors down from the room of a boy who had annoyed Iain. He waited until the house was nearly empty and pushed the boy into the cupboard from behind, bolting the door from the outside. It was over two hours before the boy was discovered.

Ciaran was often concerned that Iain might 'go native' and prefer his life, family, and friends in England and Scotland to those in his native Ireland. Ciaran need not have worried; Iain grew to despise Britain and relished deceiving those he appeared to like when secretly wishing them harm. Although Ciaran believed Iain's loyalty was to a free Ireland, he still had some doubts.

Then an act of savage brutality removed all doubts from Ciaran's mind. His sister, Chrissie, spent so much time in Strabane that she now rented a small house in the next street from her brother. In truth, she could have easily afforded a much more expensive property, but the small dwelling suited her fine and provided a bolthole where she could drink in peace. The street in which she lived was mixed; unusually, both Protestant and Catholic residents lived side by side. She soon came to the attention of the local Protestant paramilitary gang, which was intent on driving out all non-protestants from the street through a mixture of threats and abuse, which, if unsuccessful, were followed by violence. By chance, when Iain was visiting his mother, two men dressed in balaclavas petrol bombed Chrissie's house, possibly not realising that she was at home with her son. The house was full of cheap furniture, which soon went up in flames. Iain was very lucky to escape with only minor injuries, but Chrissie's burns were more severe, and she had to be rushed to hospital. Chrissie never fully recovered from this attack and she died a year later. Ciaran said it would be best for Iain not to attend the funeral.

The five years at Radley had worked perfectly for Iain and Ciaran, cementing Iain's position as an upper-class young Englishman, or Scot, with aspirations of joining the British Army. While at the school, Iain joined the CCF and started to show an interest in joining the Army. He was a bright pupil, and a place at a good university was almost a certainty. Iain was keen to apply for Trinity Dublin to read history, including Irish history. But Ciaran vetoed this idea immediately.

"I'm Irish, and I want to be a student in our capital city!" Iain would complain.

"You've got to downplay your Irish background. You're our secret weapon now. Spending three years in Dublin would ruin the picture of you we've built over the last ten years." Ciaran would counter.

Ciaran won the argument, and Iain went to Bristol University to read history. He made friends with the other public school students, some of whom he already knew from Radley. He joined the Officer Training Corps, and during the university holidays, he visited the Guards regiment, which had shown an interest in Iain as a potential officer. When he had the time, he went up to Perthshire, sometimes inviting one from his group of friends to shoot or fish. On other occasions, he would tell his friends that he was going to Scotland but, of course, not mention taking the ferry from Stranraer to meet Ciaran in Belfast.

Iain gained an upper second degree in history and shortly afterwards was selected for officer training at Victory College, the Royal Military Academy Sandhurst. The course was specially designed for potential officers who had been to university and Iain found it almost easy; nothing the College Sergeant Major bellowed was as intimidating as his early day at Sunny Meadows. Similarly, when it came to weapon training and basic tactics in the field, the standards required were childish compared to the secret training camps Ciaran had arranged for him in Ireland.

Iain passed out of Sandhurst, near the top of his intake, and reported for duty in the Guards with the battalion based in Windsor. He was an old Radleian, a graduate with a good degree, and heir to a large estate in Scotland. He had invited some of his brother officers to shoot or fish in Scotland, where they enjoyed meeting his cousin Mungo. When asked about his mother, he would say she was dead and change the subject as quickly as possible. He, of course, never spoke about his uncle, Ciaran Maguire, who was a senior intelligence officer for the IRA.

Chapter Sixteen

"You were late for the barrack guard mount. You can take an extra picket!" said Captain Iain Munro, the Assistant Adjutant. There was a faint smile on his lips, but his eyes were menacing. He was sitting behind the long table in the Orderly Room, dressed immaculately in his frock coat, complete with a gold watch chain between his two breast pockets.

Colin Smith stood to attention on the other side of the desk. "But I was on the ranges at Pirbright all day; we didn't finish firing until four p.m.," Colin replied.

"Then you should have asked for permission to leave the ranges early." Iain took his gold watch out of his blues, opened the face and glanced at the time – an unnecessary preening gesture to emphasise his position of superiority; he could have easily looked up at a large clock on the wall behind where Colin was standing that kept perfect time. "Fall Out!" ordered Iain without even looking up from his watch.

Colin could see there was no point in arguing. He saluted and left the Orderly Room. *This was so unfair!* Colin thought. It was Jeremy who had left the ranges early to make some appointments in London, leaving his entire company in Colin's care to tidy up after the ranges. He would talk to Jeremy, of course, but he was away for a week on a course, and by the time he returned to the barracks, Colin would have completed the extra picket.

Iain Munro felt very smug; he loved being nasty. Of course, he realised Jeremy hadn't given Colin enough time to return to Chelsea to mount the barrack guard, but he didn't like Colin and took pleasure in giving him any punishment, especially an unfair one. Some officers in the Battalion, such as Jeremy Kershaw, didn't like Colin Smith because he was a grammar school boy, but even Jeremy had to concede that Colin was a very capable young officer. Iain pretended that he did not like Colin for the same snobbish reasons; he even made fun of Colin because his parents lived in a house with a number while the Munro family lived in a castle. But the real reason for his displeasure was that he saw Colin as being the principal threat to his exposure as an IRA spy. Most of the other officers were blinded by the offers of shooting grouse or salmon fishing, but all this was a closed book to Colin Smith. Colin asked the exact questions that Iain wanted to avoid, and they started with his mother. Both Iain and Colin had lost their fathers and in Colin's case, he was all the more closer to his surviving mother; he had invited her to St James' Palace when he was first on Queens Guard. He was also very proud of his mother, who, despite her humble origins, had been to Oxford before qualifying as an accountant. But Iain never mentioned his dead mother for reasons about which Colin knew nothing, although he thought it was odd that Iain never brought her up in conversation.

Iain shifted uncomfortably in the adjutant's chair, recalling Colin Smith's early days in the battalion. Both Colin and Johnny Keynsham had been commissioned from Sandhurst on the same day and they had arrived in the Officers' Mess together. One night at dinner, Iain had been recounting stories of his last trip to Scotland.

"Do you shoot, Colin?" Iain had inquired, knowing full well that Colin had never fired a shotgun in his life.

"No, Iain, I've never had the chance."

"Where did you grow up?" Again, Iain knew that Colin lived in Reading.

"I was born and grew up in Reading. Where were you born, Iain?" Colin didn't know why he asked such a direct question from an officer several years his senior; he was just relieved to be the one asking the questions for once. Colin was surprised to see that his question caused Iain to redden slightly.

Colin had the sense to leave it at that, but there were other occasions when Colin asked after his mother and Iain grew nervous. Iain mentioned his disquiet, bordering on paranoia, during his regular chats with Ciaran, who had offered a brutal solution. A British officer was in the RVH recovering from a bomb attack where he had rescued an off-duty nurse; the incident made the papers and Downtown Radio had broadcast the officer's name: Colin Smith. Ciaran had quickly put together a team to murder

Colin, but the volunteers had bungled the mission, and one of them was shot and killed by Colin.

Munro took a red handkerchief from his sleeve and wiped his nose with a disdainful sniff. It was time to get ready and he had a lot to do in the evening ahead. He tidied up his desk, said a brief goodbye to the Orderly Room Colour Sergeant and walked across the square into the Officers' Mess, where he went straight to his room to change. His room was functional rather than comfortable; a single bed, a chair and a large desk, on which his Sam Browne belts – expertly polished by his orderly – lay in neat rows, ready for his inspection. Normally, he would have summoned his orderly to tell him what he needed cleaning for the following day and to give him a firm dressing down for anything that was not up to his exacting standards, but there was no time for any of that this evening. He went to a wardrobe in the corner of his room and opened the door to see his uniforms and suits all hanging neatly in accordance with the instructions he had given to Guardsman Hume. Then he changed into civilian clothes; a pin-striped suit, shirt and tie, as well as polished black brogues.

The Officers' Mess for Chelsea Barracks was at the western end of the barracks, consisting of an ugly concrete block facing Chelsea Bridge Road to its front with Pimlico Road to its west. Munro left the Officers' Mess via a small side gate, to which only the Adjutant, and the Assistant Adjutant, had the key, which led immediately to Pimlico Road.

He picked up a black cab in Holbein Mews, took it to Harrods and then entered the store and walked to the food hall. He looked at the food on offer, bought some bread and smoked salmon, and was able to check that he had not been followed before leaving from a different exit and walking swiftly to Ovington Gardens. When he arrived at number 32A, he looked like a young professional male, returning home from work and carrying his supper in the green Harrods bag. Once inside, Munro quickly made and ate some smoked salmon sandwiches; he might as well, he thought, dinner in the Officers' Mess at Chelsea would be long over by the time he had finished his evening's work.

Munro quickly looked round his house. It helped to have lots of money, he thought. He had inherited his father's businesses in Northern Ireland, which were managed by a board of directors who, as principal shareholder, he could replace at any time. However, it suited him to keep them on; provided he received the regular dividend payments – he was happy, at least for now. He had also started to transfer sums of money to a Swiss bank account in case of an emergency. His house all seemed tidy – a well-furnished sitting room, a comfortable double bedroom and a small single, all of which had been cleaned recently by his daily cleaner. *It would be nice to live here,* Munro thought briefly, but being Assistant Adjutant required him to stay in the mess, and besides, he had kept his ownership of this house very quiet to enable his secret work. He thought of it as his safe house.

Time to go to work. He opened the parcels and cases in the hall. He did not know who had left them there and he didn't care, but he noted that his house keys – which he had given to Ciaran at their last meeting – had been posted back through his letterbox. Inside the cases were all he needed for his bomb; Semtex, detonator and the timing mechanism. From his bedroom, he took a sports bag with the Royal Motorcycle Club logo on the outside and placed all the bomb-making equipment inside the bag, taking great care, particularly with the detonator. He had been taught by Ciaran's men on his secret trips to Ireland how to transport and assemble the bomb safely. Once everything was ready, he left his house, walked outside and hailed a taxi to take him to Pall Mall.

The Royal Motorcycle Club is located at 89a Pall Mall, very close to other well-known clubs in Pall Mall and St James' Street. Iain Munro had been a member of the club for a year, despite not being a very keen motorbiker. He was a keen swimmer and enjoyed the large marble swimming pool in the basement. When he walked through the tall double doors, he was full of bonhomie.

"Good evening, Russell, Are we busy?" asked Iain.

"No, sir," Russell replied. "Very quiet this evening."

Iain nodded to a couple of members who were chatting in the hall outside the bar, before descending the short staircase to the swimming pool. He went to the empty changing room, but he looked around to check that no one could see him. Very carefully, he opened his sports bag and took out his towel and trunks, which he threw on a bench beside his locker. Then, with a final look over his shoulder to check that he was not being watched, he placed the bomb-making kit in the locker and locked the door. Then he undressed, put his clothes in another empty locker – which he did not bother locking – and went for a swim, taking his towel and locker key, which he left in front of the pool while he did his lengths.

After his swim, Munro dressed and returned to Chelsea Barracks – where he had a large whisky and soda in the Officers' Mess. Munro's deadly package was secure in his locker in the RMC club, ready for action.

Chapter Seventeen

"Anyone fancy a swim?" asked Iain Munro.

"No thanks," Jeremy Kershaw replied, not bothering to look up from *The Times*, which was spread over his knees.

"What about you, grammar school boy?" Munro persisted, clearly intending to rile Colin.

"Oh, all right then," Colin replied, taking care not to show his irritation. Colin was irritated with both of his fellow officers; Munro had given him an extra picket unfairly, and Jeremy had ordered Colin to stay at Pirbright Ranges so that he would be late returning to Chelsea.

At St James' Palace, the three Guards officers were sitting in the Queen's Guard Officers' Mess. They had mounted guard that morning; lunch had finished, and there was little to do until drinks in the evening.

"Since when were you so keen on swimming?" Jeremy asked, not sounding very interested even in his own question.

"I've always liked swimming in the sea or even in a lake," Iain replied.

"You must be mad to swim in Scotland. Bloody freezing."

"Or in Ireland," added Colin.

Again, Colin noticed Iain's face reddening just very slightly at the mention of Ireland.

Colin and Iain went up to their rooms to get ready for their swim. One of the perks of being on guard at St James' was using the swimming pool at the RMC Club, which is a short walk away in Pall Mall. Officers on guard leaving the palace had to be in full uniform, even for the short walk to the RMC Club, according to the rules. Colin put on his tunic, which was still warm inside from the guard mount, strapped on his sword and sash, and put on his white gloves. Before leaving his room, he collected a towel and a pair of swimming trunks from his case and made his way down one flight of stairs to wait for Munro. On the first floor landing, the three bearskins for each of the three officers were on stands in a neat row. Colin grabbed his bearskin and put his towel and trunks inside the cap before placing his bearskin carefully on his head. A moment later, Munro came clattering down the stairs, also in full guard order, without his bearskin.

"Do you like my new trunks?" asked Munro, waving a pair of bright orange swimmers in Colin's face.

"Yes, very smart, perhaps a bit bright," Colin replied.

"Well, I like them; come on, let's go," said Munro eagerly, shoving his swimming gear deep inside his bearskin.

Before turning into Pall Mall, the two Guards officers set off into Marlborough Road, nodding a friendly greeting to the policeman on duty. In less than two minutes, they were on the steps of the RMC Club and nodded another friendly greeting to the Hall Porter. Munro noted that today it was not Russell on duty but another porter, Peter, who paid little attention to the officers going for a swim.

Peter was busy, in any case, helping a couple of members find their coats after what had obviously been a very good lunch.

Munro nearly burst into the changing room in the basement of the club. "Member lockers are this way, but you can change over there," said Munro archly.

Colin found himself opening a medium-sized locker; he undressed carefully, and there was enough room inside it just to hang up his uniform beside his bearskin. Once changed, Colin went to the pool where Munro was already doing his lengths; he was a very good swimmer, slicing up and down the pool in an easy crawl. Colin thought there was something slightly comic and obscene about Munro's bright orange trunks sticking up above the waterline. Unlike Munro, Colin was not a particularly strong swimmer, and he eased himself gently into the pool down some steps and then began a steady breaststroke, trying to avoid the wake from Munro's crawl. Colin was soon bored, so he lifted himself out of the pool and sat on a bench to dry himself with a towel.

"Had enough already?" shouted Munro from the pool.

"Yes, I think I'll head back to the mess," Colin replied.

"Catch you later; I've got another ten lengths to go!" Munro thrust his head into the water and resumed his purposeful crawl.

God, you're a bore! Colin wanted to reply but kept his thoughts to himself as he made his way back to the changing room. He was thankful to be by himself, if only for a short while, and to have a chance to think about the past few days and the evening ahead. Since that fantastic night with Mary at his sister's party, Colin had only had one chance to see her again when their lovemaking had been slower and more tender. But, with Munro's extra pickets and guard duties, Colin found it very difficult to make the time to travel to Sarah's rented house in Kilburn. Sarah and Mary had become good friends, and recently Mary moved into her house that was full of other students. However, both of them were now busy medical students working very long hours at Imperial College and spent less and less time in their Kilburn house, and even when they did, catching a few hours of precious sleep was the priority.

Meanwhile, Munro continued swimming for another five minutes. Then he left the pool and did a quick search of the changing rooms to check that Colin had left. Munro dried himself and put on his pants and trousers; then he unlocked and opened his member's locker. Everything inside was as he had left it the evening before, much to his relief. Munro started sweating slightly and he could feel his pulse rate quicken. Next, he removed the bomb and explosive from the locker and very carefully packed it inside his bearskin; he had practised this many times in his London house. He was going to have to leave his towel and swimming trunks in the locker, as there would not be enough room for them besides the bomb. In any case, he didn't want anything wet or even damp next to the bomb. On his way to the club, Munro had worn a sweatshirt under his tunic, and this would also be left in the locker for the return journey; in its place, Munro had prepared another sweatshirt with specially fitted pockets containing the detonators, some wiring and the timing mechanism. Munro was very fit and slender, and he knew he could fit his special sweatshirt under his tunic. Again, he had practised this beforehand. It was time to go, and Munro finished his dressing. He was nervous now and did not look forward to the short walk back to St James'. To all appearances, he looked like the perfect Guards officer; gleaming boots, red tunic with sword and sash, white gloves and his bearskin. There was nothing to prove that he wore a special vest under his tunic or that the contents inside his bearskin were deadly. Munro said a brief farewell to the hall porter as he left the RMC Club, turned left, and headed back towards St James'.

Munro was nervous; carrying detonators was always dangerous, and he had been told of volunteers who had blown off their hands when trying to assemble bombs. He walked at a slower pace than usual, anxious not to disrupt his dangerous cargo, but he was glad to be walking alone at his speed.

When Munro arrived back at St James', he pressed the buzzer outside the entrance to Queen's Guard.

"It's the Subaltern, returning from the RMC Club," said Munro into the speaker, and he was relieved when the door was promptly buzzed open by the duty sergeant. Munro made his way up the steep flight of stairs to the landing, where both Kershaw's and Colin's bearskins were neatly set out on stands on the table outside the main mess room. Normally, Munro would have placed his bearskin on the stand reserved for the subaltern, but on this occasion, keeping his bearskin firmly on his head, Munro went straight up to his bedroom, closed the door behind him, and moved quickly. Carefully, he removed his bearskin and laid it on the bed, with its contents facing away from the door in case he was disturbed. Next, he took off his tunic and his special vest, noting with relief that the equipment packed into the vest appeared to be in order, and he laid these on the bed beside his bearskin. From under his bed, he took out an empty suitcase, placed the contents of his bearskin inside, together with his special vest, closed the case, locked it and put it back under his bed. Nothing of his bomb was visible now, but he had a couple of touches to make to protect his cover. From a drawer, he took out a pair of bright orange swimming trunks and a towel identical to what he had taken to the RMC Club earlier. He walked over to his basin, soaked the trunks, wrapped them in his towel, and put them inside his bearskin for a moment before placing both towel and trunks on his basin. Putting on a collarless white shirt and still dressed in his blue trousers, he picked up his bearskin and a spare curb chain and walked down the flight of stairs to the first landing, where the other two bearskins were laid out.

Munro wanted to have an explanation for taking his bearskin up to his room rather than leaving it on its stand on the first landing, as usual. When he reached the landing, he saw Colin making a telephone call from the pay phone in the alcove behind the bearskins.

"Just been fitting a new curb chain on my bearskin," said Munro loudly enough for Colin to hear and Jeremy too if he was still reading in the mess next door. Then Munro placed his bearskin alongside the two others and went back upstairs to change for evening drinks.

Colin could not have cared less about Munro's curb chain or anything else about Munro. What he did care about was whether his sister, Sarah, and her housemate, Mary, were going to come for drinks later that evening. There was no reply to the shared phone in their house; that was no surprise; it could ring for ages sometimes before a passing student bothered to answer. Colin wondered if they had both already left for St James' or forgotten about his invitation. Both explanations were possible. He sighed, replaced the phone handle and wandered next door to the main mess room, where Jeremy was also on the telephone. Jeremy was on the military phone situated on a small cabinet in the corner of the room next to the regimental colour. It was difficult to make civilian calls on the military network but Jeremy, as Captain of the Guard, had found a way.

"Excellent. See you here at eight p.m.," Jeremy was saying, "Yes, black tie. Bye."

Jeremy turned towards Colin. "Just checking on my brother. He can come to dinner but won't be here until just before eight p.m., working hard in the city as usual. My mother and my aunt are coming for a drink before we dine."

Colin nodded. He liked Richard Kershaw, whom he had met on Queen's Guard earlier that year but had not met Jeremy's mother or his aunt. It was time to get ready for drinks to be followed by dinner and both Jeremy and Colin went upstairs to change. Munro was in his room and had already changed but had other, more lethal, preparations to make. The main bomb containing the Semtex explosive, which had been carried inside his bearskin, was already prepared. The most difficult part, the fitting of the timing mechanism and the detonators, had yet to be done. This was also the most dangerous part, but Munro had practised this both at a secret training camp in Ireland and in his London home. He laid the main bomb on his bed behind a suitcase that should hide it if he was unexpectedly disturbed. *Just my luck if the bloody grammar school boy was to walk in now,* he thought.

Gingerly, he inserted the detonator into the Semtex and attached the timing mechanism. Once it was ready, Munro was sweating again. *I should have done this in my pants before changing!* he thought. From under his bed, he took out a large blue paper bag, the sort given to customers in expensive shops in which to take home their purchases. After setting the timer, he placed the bomb in the bag and walked downstairs to the mess room. As he had expected, both the Captain of the Guard and the Ensign were changing in their rooms, and the mess sergeant was in the kitchen area. But even if anyone had been in the mess room, he had some nonsense prepared about leaving a parcel for his orderly to collect. Everyone knew how tough he was on his orderly and this explanation would be readily believed. In the event, the mess room was empty and the dining table had already been laid out for dinner at eight p.m., so Munro entered swiftly and walked over to the corner where the regimental colour was on display next to the military telephone. Behind the telephone, there was a small space between the cabinet and the wall of the mess that was just big enough to provide a hiding place for the bomb. Removing the paper bag, Munro took one last look at the timer before gently sliding the bomb behind the telephone's cabinet. He had done all that he could and after checking that nothing of the bomb was visible, he went upstairs to his room, taking the paper bag with him.

"Been shopping, Iain?" asked Colin, who passed Munro on the stairs.

"Looking for my bloody orderly," Munro muttered, thinking how much he wanted Colin to be killed by the bomb; then his nosy questions would stop.

Colin did not care at all about Munro's shopping bag or his orderly, but he did notice that Munro seemed particularly irritable since he had returned from his swim. Colin entered the mess and asked the mess sergeant to bring him tonic water with lemon and plenty of ice. He was nervous and wanted to stay sober before his guests arrived, assuming they had even remembered. Jeremy entered shortly afterwards and ordered a large gin and tonic.

The mess sergeant came in with the drinks. "Excuse me, sir, your guests are here."

Colin had hoped to see Sarah and Mary but turned to see that instead two elderly ladies had entered the mess; they were both short, well-dressed, and looked nearly identical. Colin could see a resemblance to someone he knew, and he then realised that one was Jeremy's mother and the other her sister.

"Hello Mother. Hello, Aunt Muriel," said Jeremy, looking a little subdued as he kissed both of them rather formally.

"Colin, may I introduce you to my mother, Susan, and my aunt, Muriel Greville?"

The four of them shook hands and said hello to each other. Colin noticed that Munro had not yet joined them, and Jeremy was not pleased.

"I've wanted so much to meet you, Colin. Jeremy has told me all about you. How are you finding life in the regiment?" asked Susan Kershaw.

Colin felt awkward with Jeremy standing next to his mother.

"I'm enjoying myself very much," Colin replied not untruthfully, although he might have added 'now' to the end of his reply.

"Jeremy tells me you were nearly killed rescuing a young girl after a bomb," Susan Kershaw continued. "Apparently, it was all in the papers. Did you know who she was?"

"Mary Flynn," A quiet voice spoke from behind them. They all turned towards the door where Mary was standing.

"I'm sorry, dear, and you are?" Susan Kershaw asked gently.

"Mary Flynn," Mary replied, moving to Colin's side and putting one arm around his waist. "I met Colin at the Royal."

Her brief stay in London had only slightly softened her Irish accent. She was wearing a light blue dress that fitted her like a glove; it looked familiar, and Colin guessed that she had borrowed it from his sister, Sarah. A brief and awkward silence followed, which was interrupted by Sarah cheerfully and busily introducing herself to everyone. "Hello, I'm Sarah, Colin's sister, and this is my housemate Mary; we're studying medicine together at Imperial!" Susan Kershaw and her sister, Muriel, were taken aback by the flood of new information that had been offered to them in less than a minute. "Hello, Jeremy," Sarah continued, "do you remember me? I met you at lunch here with my mother."

"I do remember," Jeremy replied, looking a little pale. "I trust your mother is well."

At this moment, Iain Munro appeared, looking flushed and out of breath. "Sorry, I'm late," he said.

Jeremy did not look pleased, but he introduced Munro to his mother and aunt.

It was Colin's turn. "May I introduce my sister Sarah and—"

"Iain Munro, a pleasure," Munro replied loudly before Colin could finish his introduction and shook Sarah's hand a bit too firmly. He then grasped Mary's hand. "Iain Munro," he repeated gruffly. "Mary Flynn," Mary replied quietly.

"The Mary Flynn from Belfast?" asked Munro rudely. There was another silence.

Unexpectedly, this time, it was Jeremy who came to the rescue. "Iain, my mother has just returned from Scotland, not far from your estate." Iain moved over to talk to Susan Kershaw and the small drinks party now formed into two groups; Jeremy, his mother, his aunt and Munro talked together while, a few feet away, Colin, Mary and Sarah chatted away happily. This suited everyone fine until at eight p.m. sharp, the Mess Sergeant lit the candles on the dining table, signalling that dinner was ready and that it was time for the ladies to depart.

Mary gave Munro a curious look as she left the Queen's Guard Mess. She had not seen the way Munro had stared at her earlier – a look of intense hatred.

Chapter Eighteen

"Would you like another glass of brandy, Richard?" asked Jeremy Kershaw.

"No thanks; I should be going soon," his brother replied.

There were three of them sitting around the dining table in the Queen's Guard Officers' Mess; Jeremy, his brother Richard and Colin. Munro had left the dinner fifteen minutes earlier to check on the guard at Buckingham Palace itself, where, as the Subaltern, he would be spending the night. It had not been necessary for Munro to leave the dinner so early; his checking of the sentries could have waited another half an hour and Jeremy had thought of saying so. But, in truth, he was glad Munro had left the dinner early; he had spoiled what would otherwise have been a very pleasant evening. *Why had Munro been so rude to Colin's guests?* Jeremy wondered, *And then, during dinner, he was so loud and drinking more than normal.* However, once Munro had left, the three that remained were able to relax and their conversation flowed.

Munro, on the other hand, was very relieved to be out of St James' and walking across the park to Buckingham Palace. He needed some fresh air to clear his head and calm his nerves. He knew he had annoyed Jeremy at dinner, but the bomb preparation and its planting had got to Munro. Sitting down to dinner with Jeremy and his brother, not to mention Colin, that nosy grammar school boy, had been too much. Then Munro worried the timer might be faulty and that the bomb might explode while he was still in the mess. Hopefully, the bomb would explode in a matter of minutes, kill two Army officers and strike a blow for a free Ireland!

It was important now that nothing could link him to the bomb. He carried a small briefcase and was dressed in his tunic, wearing a forage cap instead of the bearskin that would be worn in daylight. It was unremarkable for the Subaltern to carry a small case, perhaps containing a book and overnight things, for the short walk in the dark from St James' to Buckingham Palace. Munro's case, however, carried his bomb-making equipment and the special vest he had worn from the RMC Club to St James'. He had to dispose of the briefcase, which contained the last few items that could link Munro to the bomb.

Brendan Flynn felt silly and uncomfortable in a dinner jacket. But Chloe had insisted that this was what was required, and he had no choice other than to comply. Ciaran had made it very clear back in Strabane that Chloe was the operational commander while they were on the UK mainland. Brendan did not like this, but he realised he had to accept it – how he longed to be back in Ireland, fighting his war in his way, and preferably in Co Tyrone.

Chloe was also dressing up for the event and, unlike Brendan, she found this easy as she enjoyed playing the role of a carefree young English girl on a night out in London. She wore a long blue dress over her slender figure, with bangles and bracelets over both wrists and a small silver crucifix around her neck. She also carried a large bag made of coloured patches that were both tatty and stylish at the same time. It was the sort of bag an overland traveller might have picked up in Asia, and an onlooker might have guessed that this pretty young girl had changed for her date in her office and that her work clothes were in the bag. Fortunately for Chloe, no one asked to look inside her bag, and if they had, they would have seen a small jacket and a blouse that she might have worn in an office. Hopefully, they would not have seen the small briefcase hidden underneath her clothes that was identical to Munro's briefcase.

Munro had been told by Ciaran to stop at the park bench to the left of the path that ran from St James' to the pedestrian lights at the eastern end of Constitution Hill. He stopped as he had been told to tie up the laces on his George boots and to leave his briefcase beside the bench. Munro was relieved to see the identical briefcase beside the bench, which had been placed there a few minutes earlier by Brendan and Chloe. He did not know who had made the drop and he did not want to know. Once Munro had finished with the show of tying up his laces, he picked up the identical case, leaving his own by the bench, and walked slowly towards Buckingham Palace without once looking back.

Chloe had decided that Brendan and she should pretend to be a couple at the start of a love affair. They had been to a bar in Mayfair earlier, where they both allowed themselves one alcoholic and several soft drinks. Brendan noted that there were other customers in the bar wearing dinner jackets and this made him feel part of the crowd. When it was time, they both left the bar, arm in arm and walked south to Piccadilly, which they crossed at Green Park underground and then continued south through Green Park, keeping St James' Palace on their left. There was lots of giggling and flirting from Chloe, to which Brendan responded hesitantly at first and then more warmly as he relaxed into the role he had to play. When they arrived at the bench, Chloe dropped the bag on the ground, and they started to kiss before Chloe turned to open the bag, taking out a small mirror and some lipstick that she applied to her lips.

"Look what you've done to my lips, you beast!" she laughed.

Once finished, she put the mirror and lipstick back in the bag and removed the briefcase, which she left beside the bench.

"Come on, race you to the top!" challenged Chloe, who started running back towards Piccadilly. Brendan ran after her and when they reached Piccadilly, they wandered towards a club in Berkeley Square that let them in and where they had another drink. They had been told to wait another ten minutes before heading back south into the park and sitting on the same bench. They then went through a similar process of giggling, kissing and taking various items in and out of the bag, which made it easy for Chloe to place Munro's briefcase in the bag. Shortly afterwards, they stood up and headed towards Piccadilly for the final time, just before a passing policeman was about to ask the noisy young couple to move on.

This was the last mission set for Brendan and Chloe on the UK mainland. Brendan was delighted to be returning to Ireland, in his case, via a ferry from Liverpool to Belfast. Ciaran wanted Chloe back in Belfast as quickly as possible, and she had been ordered to take the first flight from Heathrow to Aldergrove the next morning.

Sergeant Appleby put down the telephone in the Buckingham Palace guardroom and swore.

"Fucking hell, why does Captain Munro want to inspect the sentries so bloody early?" He would have liked to say much more about Mr Munro, but in front of the two junior guardsmen who were waiting to go on duty, there was a limit to how much he could openly criticise an officer. Instead, he limited himself to saying, "Subaltern's round in five minutes; get fucking ready!"

As Sergeant Appleby quickly made the preparations for Munro's arrival, it struck him that he did not like the Assistant Adjutant, Captain Munro. This was odd because he liked most of the other officers in the Battalion and he knew he was popular with them as well; he had just been selected to be a platoon colour sergeant at Sandhurst next year, which would mean both promotion and a sign that his career was heading in the right direction. Major

Kershaw was a stickler, but he knew how to command a company. Everyone liked Mr Keynsham, of course, but he was always losing his equipment, himself, and his platoon. Appleby's favourite was Mr Smith, or Colin, as he was known, but not to his face. But Appleby could see Colin's difficulty fitting in with some of the others in the Officers' Mess. Appleby's thoughts were interrupted by the abrupt arrival of Captain Munro, who was scowling and out of breath.

"Anything to report?" Munro, demanded.

"No, sir." Sergeant Appleby gave Munro an immaculate salute, adding calmly, "We're ready for the rounds when you are, sir."

In the Queen's Guard Officers' Mess, the telephone rang shrilly. Jeremy Kershaw was saying goodbye to his brother and standing nearest to the telephone.

"Captain of the Guard," answered Jeremy formally.

"Put me on to Colin Smith!" The accent was pure Belfast, and the voice was insistent. It was a woman's voice.

"Who's speaking?" Jeremy sounded irritated.

"Mister, you put me on to wee Colin, now!"

Although getting angry, Jeremy handed the phone to Colin. "It's for you," he said lamely.

Colin put the receiver to his ear. "Is that you, Colin?" The strong Belfast accent sounded aggressive and alien standing in the Queen's Guard Officers' Mess.

"Yes, but who—"

The woman's voice interrupted. "There's a bomb! You get out, now Colin!" And the line went dead.

Colin turned to find Jeremy and his brother staring at him. "She said there's a bomb! "We must call ATO."

"The emergency numbers are on the sheet by the telephone!" said Jeremy, who was starting to spit – a sign that he was worried.

Colin looked for the laminated sheet of paper with the list of emergency numbers that should be beside the telephone. It must have fallen behind the desk when Jeremy or Munro used the telephone earlier that evening.

"Hang on, there's something here!" Colin shouted, and without thinking, he reached behind the desk where he could see the sheet of telephone numbers and a strange package to its side. He lifted both up, walked over to the dining table and dropped them in the centre next to the port decanter and the cigar box. Jeremy and Richard Kershaw stared at the table without speaking; the package was clearly a bomb with what looked like sticks of Semtex and a timing device bound tightly together with black masking tape. Colin reacted first. He walked over to the large French windows that opened to the terrace on top of the guardroom roof, then he grabbed the mysterious package, laid it gently on the roof and walked back inside.

"I think we should clear the building now, Jeremy!" said Colin urgently, but he was surprised at how calm his voice sounded.

Jeremy had now taken in the situation. "Evacuate the building now!"

Jeremy's brother was practically forced out of the building, as were the few remaining mess staff. Once they were downstairs and outside, Colin ran into the guardroom to evacuate the building. This was easy; when everyone heard that there was a bomb on the guardroom roof, no one waited around to ask questions. Meanwhile, Jeremy had alerted the policeman on duty in Ambassador's Court and requested urgent help including an ATO (a bomb disposal officer). Ambassador's Court was filled with people, mainly the guardroom occupants, but a few from Clarence House, where fortunately none of the Royal Family were in residence. Police appeared from nowhere, and very shortly, a man in army uniform – a captain who was evidently the ATO – asked who had found the suspect bomb.

"I did," said Colin. The last time Colin had spoken to an ATO was in Belfast.

"Tell me what happened," The ATO persisted without wasting time on introductions.

"There was a telephone call, a bomb warning and then I saw something odd behind the table, which I lifted out and put on the roof."

"You moved what looked like a bomb," the ATO was angry. "You f…"

But no one heard the rest of the ATO's sentence as a very loud explosion rocked the nearby buildings. Everyone in Ambassador's Court threw themselves to the ground and was promptly covered by showers of broken glass.

Chapter Nineteen

"What in the name of Jesus went wrong, Iain?" Ciaran demanded.

"How should I know?" Munro replied morosely. "In fact, I did everything as we agreed to the fucking letter."

Ciaran Maguire looked at Iain Munro sharply. It was unusual for Munro to swear, and he was clearly upset. They had called a crash meeting at a pub in Castle Douglas, Dumfriesshire. This was convenient for both of them. Munro could make a minor detour on his way up to Perthshire, and Ciaran took the Bangor to Stranraer ferry with enough time to return to Northern Ireland the same day. The pub had seen better days with only a few customers, but it was quiet, which enabled the two of them to have a long chat. There was plenty to discuss.

Munro had heard the bomb explode from the forecourt of Buckingham Palace where he was making his rounds. He had rushed back to the guardroom at the southern end of the forecourt, where the telephones were all ringing. News came in that a bomb had exploded in St James' Palace and Munro was secretly delighted but his delight turned to dismay when he heard that no one had been killed or seriously injured.

"I thought the plan was not to telephone a warning until after the bomb had exploded. Why the change of plan?" asked Munro.

"We didn't give a fucking telephone warning! We only claimed responsibility after the bomb had exploded," Ciaran hissed, trying to keep his voice down.

"Well, someone bloody did! And whoever it was, she spoke to Colin Smith."

"She? We don't use a bloody woman to give bomb warnings."

"Smith was sure it was a woman and she asked to speak to Colin Smith."

"Colin Smith?" Ciaran paused. "The officer from the RVH?"

"Yes, the nosy Colin Smith, who's always asking me awkward questions about my past. Your team in Belfast was supposed to kill him when he was a sitting duck in the RVH."

Iain Munro and Ciaran Maguire continued their secret conversation, which would have become heated if it were not for the fact that they did not want to draw attention to themselves. Ciaran was concerned about the mysterious bomb warning as well as the possibility that Munro would be under suspicion. But Munro was confident that he was not suspected and that the elaborate means of bringing the bomb into the palace and the removal of the bomb-making equipment had gone smoothly. After a while, the two plotters calmed down, and Ciaran went to the bar to order another round of beers.

Munro waited until Ciaran returned to their table with their drinks and sat down. Then Munro leant towards him across the table. "I do have some good news," he whispered.

In truth, neither side was happy about the bomb attack at St James' Palace. The IRA leadership was furious that such an elaborate plan that stretched their resources had caused no serious casualties, while the security forces were shocked that the IRA had managed to set off a bomb within St James' Palace. The telephone bomb warning confounded the security forces every bit as much as it did the IRA. The fact that the caller had insisted on speaking to Colin Smith added to the mystery. Colin received little praise for finding the bomb and was criticised for his recklessness in moving it onto the terrace outside the mess, even though the damage would have been greater had the bomb exploded in its original position.

In the days that followed the bomb, Colin faced serious questioning, which was every bit as intense as the grilling that he had endured following the RVH shooting in Belfast. To make matters worse, this time it was not just the military police asking the questions. The Metropolitan Police were in charge of the incident, and a chief inspector working in counterterrorism put Colin through a series of tough interviews. Colin was asked about everything in the days leading up to guard duty and his routine on the guard itself. His interviewers were particularly interested in his guests for drinks, not his sister so much, but special attention was given to Mary Flynn, his new girlfriend.

Colin answered all the questions truthfully and fully, and he had no option but to explain how he had met Mary in the Ardoyne and the events that had followed in the RVH. Colin soon realised the police considered him a suspect, or at least complicit, in the bomb attack planning. Meeting Mary at his sister's student party was an unplanned coincidence that cut little ice with his interrogators.

Colin was confined to Chelsea Barracks in the weeks following the bomb attack. The police wanted him in the cells of the Wood Street police station but, rather unexpectedly, Jeremy had come to Colin's aid. He delayed his holiday to Umbria, and with the help of his brother, he managed to find a criminal barrister who persuaded the police that custody would not be necessary if Colin stayed within the barracks. In between sessions with counter-terrorism officers and the military police, Colin had little to do in Chelsea Barracks. The battalion was embarking on block leave and the barracks was emptying fast, leaving only a small rear party to keep the base secure for the next two weeks. Some of the officers had already departed, including Munro, who had left for his estate in Perthshire. Colin did not miss Munro, but he would have liked to hear his version of events after he had left the dinner. As it was, Munro was free to go on holiday, while Colin was effectively a prisoner within Chelsea Barracks.

Colin wanted to speak to his mother, who was on holiday in Tuscany, and he tried calling her hotel several times from the telephone in the Officers' Mess, where there was little privacy. When he eventually managed to speak to her, the mess was nearly empty, and he was able to give her a brief explanation about what had happened and his present situation. The bomb incident in St James' Palace had been mentioned briefly on the news in Italy, but fortunately, his mother had no idea how close her son had been to the explosion. When she heard that Colin was under investigation, she was both very shocked and worried and wanted to end her holiday immediately to give Colin whatever help she could. However, Colin was able to persuade her to finish her holiday, as there was very little that she could do to help.

Colin rang his sister's student house repeatedly where the telephone seemed to ring endlessly without answer. Eventually, he did manage to reach Sarah, who sounded worried, and Colin guessed that she had been speaking to her mother. Colin did all that he could to reassure his sister, who was in the middle of exams and he did not want to disturb her. He, of course, asked to speak to Mary, but Sarah said that this was not possible. Apparently, Mary's mother was very ill, and Mary had had to rush back to Northern Ireland to see her. Sarah didn't have a telephone number for Mary and if she was staying with her mother in Strabane, the likelihood was that there was no telephone in the house anyway. The university would have her details, but Colin felt he could not ask Sarah to approach them in the middle of her exams.

A week after the bomb attack, there was a rare piece of good news for Colin. After completing his platoon commander's course at Warminster, Johnny Keynsham returned to the battalion. They were both delighted to see each other and, as it happened, they were both in need of some good cheer. Johnny's course had not gone well, and he had managed to lose both his platoon and a box of live ammunition on the final exercise. He had been told to report to the commanding officer the next day to hear his course report, and he was not looking forward to this interview.

The Officers' Mess at Chelsea was nearly empty when Colin and Johnny went to dinner in the evening. They both tried to be optimistic and spoke about the forthcoming battalion 'block leave'. Johnny was going to spend a few days with his parents at Keynsham outside Cheltenham before flying off to Corfu with his two sisters and some of their fast friends. Johnny was keen for Colin to join them, but he could hardly accept his friend's kind offer when his immediate future was so uncertain.

At six o'clock the following morning, Colin went for his customary run around the barracks. He would have liked to have run out of the front gate, crossed Chelsea Bridge and have a good stretch in Battersea Park. He wistfully looked at the front gate as he ran past and noticed an army Land Rover pull up outside the guardroom. After a couple of laps, Colin cut short his run and made his way back to the mess; he had promised to make sure Johnny was up early in good time for his interview with the commanding officer. Colin ran into the front of the mess and sprinted up the first flight of steps to a large landing with the main mess and dining room to his right and the

TV room to his left. He was surprised to see Johnny standing there, already dressed, and looking anxious. He was then astonished when Jeremy also appeared in full service dress, looking very serious and not his usual haughty self.

"The military police will be here any minute," said Jeremy without any preamble. "I've come to give you a bit of warning. They want to continue their interviews at the barracks in Hounslow. I've spoken to the commanding officer, and you've got to do what they say."

Colin could hear voices coming from the front entrance to the mess below where they were standing. He remembered seeing the army land rover pulling up outside the guardroom during his run. Within moments, two members of the military police in service dress and still wearing their red hats stood at the top of the stairs to face Colin, Johnny and Jeremy. One of the pair was none other than Captain Sarah Matthews, whom Colin had last encountered in the aftermath of the RVH shooting in Belfast.

Captain Matthews looked directly at Colin. "You're to come with us immediately," she ordered.

"I thought the Royal Military Police saluted a senior officer," said Jeremy quietly but firmly.

"I'm sorry, sir," both Captain Matthews and her sergeant saluted. Colin noticed that their salutes were very smart and would have passed muster on the drill square. They made an impressive pair. Captain Matthews looked both efficient in a bossy sort of way and alluring at the same time. Her sergeant was over six feet tall and looked as if he had been carved out of a concrete bunker.

"I have orders from the Major General commanding London District that Mr Smith is to come with us." This time she looked at Jeremy, who nodded.

"Yes, we were told to expect you," said Jeremy.

A couple of young officers walked down the stairs on their way to breakfast. They walked past the group and entered the dining room. From inside, someone said, "What are those two monkeys doing in the Officers' Mess?"

"Can you at least tell me what is going on?" asked Colin.

"No, I can't," Captain Matthews replied firmly. "And we need to get going. Sergeant Hansen, do you have the list?"

"Yes ma'am." The sergeant reached inside his service dress jacket, brought out a white sheet of paper and handed it to Colin.

"Go and pack what's on the list and nothing else," Captain Matthews ordered. Sergeant Hansen started to follow Colin upstairs to his room, but Jeremy intervened.

"Wait. I suggest Lord Keynsham escorts Mr Smith to his room to pack. He'll make sure he doesn't abscond."

Colin and Johnny rushed up the stairs to his room, leaving Captain Matthews, Sergeant Hansen and Jeremy outside the anteroom. The sound of a young officer imitating a monkey could be heard from where they were standing.

"I think it might be best if we wait for Mr Smith at the front entrance to the mess," said Jeremy tactfully, leading the two military police downstairs.

Once inside his room, Colin sat on his bed with a sigh. "What on earth is all this about? I've answered all their bloody questions! Why am I being picked on? Jeremy and Munro were on guard as well as me. All because I have an Irish girlfriend."

"Well, wherever you're going, you will be even fitter than you are now," said Johnny, who had taken the list from Colin and was reading it with a puzzled look.

"Looks like you'll be having a fun time," Johnny continued. "PT kit times three, plimsolls, denim trousers, tracksuit – do you actually have a tracksuit?"

"Yes, I've got a tracksuit, not that I've dared to wear it in Chelsea Barracks."

Colin took down a suitcase from the top of his cupboard and dropped it on his bed. He opened it and started packing.

"What about civvies?" Colin asked as he bundled his PT kit into the case.

"Well yes, but not the order of dress for a Guards officer; two pairs of jeans, a thick jumper and an anorak," replied Johnny, who rarely wore jeans and didn't even own an anorak.

The packing didn't take long because the list was so short and Colin quickly changed into combat dress again as instructed by the sheet of paper. As they left Colin's room, Colin handed Johnny the keys to his car. "Please don't lose these, Johnny. When you go on leave, take the BMW to Keynsham if you want."

Captain Matthews and Sergeant Hansen were waiting outside the mess beside an army Land Rover, which Colin guessed was the vehicle he saw by the guardroom earlier.

"Get in, "said Captain Matthews. "We're in a hurry."

"What time did you book our table?" asked Colin with a deadpan expression.

Sarah Matthews barely looked at Colin and got into the front seat of the Land Rover next to the driver.

Colin went round to the back of the land rover to climb inside, but Sergeant Hansen stood in his way. "Let me give you some advice, sir. Less of the funny one-liners. Won't do you any good where you're going."

"That's my problem; I don't know where I'm going because no one will tell me anything."

Sergeant Hansen stood to one side and Colin climbed into the back of the land rover, which trundled out of the front gate, turned right, headed onto Sloane Square and then took the exit for King's Road. After a while, Colin began to wonder what route they were going to take to Hounslow when the land rover suddenly turned left off the King's Road and into Duke of York barracks. Colin had never been to this barracks before and knew little about what went on inside other than it was the base for a reserve SAS regiment. There seemed to be very few people around, and no one was in uniform, making it impossible to tell who was who. The Land Rover pulled up outside a nondescript barrack hut, and both Sergeant Hansen and Captain Matthews climbed out.

"Follow me," said Captain Matthews to Colin, who was still sitting in the back of the vehicle, waiting to be told what was going to happen next. Colin followed her into the building, which was a long wooden hut all on ground level with a corridor running its length and small offices to its side. At the end of the corridor, there was a closed door on which Sarah Matthews knocked twice and a man's voice from inside told her to enter. Both Sarah and Colin entered what was another small office with a desk, two chairs and a metal filing cabinet. There were no papers on the desk, and there was nothing anywhere to indicate who used the office. Colin found himself facing the so-called Major Smith, who stood on the other side of the empty desk with his back to a window that looked out on what could be a drill square. Major Smith, or Grenville, was dressed in combat dress; his jacket looked a little too big for him, and he wore the crossed swords and crown of a lieutenant general on his shoulders. The overall impression was of short-term necessity – a borrowed office and a borrowed uniform that would both be discarded when no longer required.

"Congratulations on your promotion, sir," Colin saluted. "When we met in Belfast, you were only a major."

"Shut up and sit down," came the short reply.

Both men sat down to face each other across the empty desk. Sarah Matthews left the room, closing the door quietly behind her.

"My name and rank are none of your business and are not important," said the man who, until a moment ago, Colin believed to be Major Smith. "But what matters is what I do with you. Let me sum things up. Your girlfriend comes from Strabane, her siblings are IRA, you survive a shooting in the RVH, which looks more like an assassination and you invite your girlfriend to bloody drinks in St James' Palace!"

"Mary is not in the IRA!" Colin protested.

"How can you be so bloody sure?" A helicopter was landing on the drill square and Major Smith had to shout to be heard. "And then, you get a bomb warning on the telephone, personal for Colin Smith; no one else will do!"

"I didn't ask to be shot at or bombed," Colin replied.

"Maybe not, but drama follows you wherever you go. Second Lieutenant Smith, you are trouble – big trouble – but from now on, you are my trouble. Get out."

Sarah Matthews opened the door, and Colin followed her back down along the corridor and outside, where Sergeant Hansen stood waiting. Both of them wore combat dress and looked serious. Sarah Matthews told Colin to follow as they ran not towards the land rover but towards the Wessex helicopter, which stood waiting on the drill square with its engines running.

Chapter Twenty

Before they left Green Park on the night of the explosion, Chloe had given Brendan strict instructions. He was to dispose of the bag, make his way to a safe house and be ready to leave the UK the next day. But Brendan ignored all this and instead managed to find a pub that was still open and proceeded to get drunk. He soon started to be abusive, and the landlord was glad to close up. Brendan found himself on the street in an alcoholic haze and decided, on a whim, to call in on his sister.

Mary Flynn had enjoyed the short drinks party at the St James' Palace Officers' Mess, or at least she had, until that arrogant Brit started being so rude. Something about him, not just his behaviour, unsettled her, and she thought she may have met him before, although heaven knows where. He couldn't have been with her when she was growing up in Strabane. Sarah had left the party at the same time but was now going to have some supper with her mother, who had been in London for the day. As a result, Mary made her way back to the shared student house alone. As she was about to enter, she was astonished to find her brother Brendan sitting in the dark on the doorstep; he had obviously been drinking heavily.

"Holy Mother of God! Brendan, what are you doing here?"

"Thought I'd come round and meet my little sis for a drink."

"Looks as if you've had a few already." Mary hated being called sis. "We don't have any of the hard stuff; maybe coffee. Get up off the doorstep."

Mary opened the door with her key and made her way into the small kitchen, turning on the light. Brendan shambled in after her and sat heavily on a kitchen chair. He had a large bag with him, which he dropped on the kitchen floor with a thud. As she put the kettle on the stove, Mary thought guiltily that she was glad none of her housemates were around to see her brother, especially after a drinking spell. She turned to look at her brother.

"Dear Jesus, Brendan, look at the state of you all dressed up in suits and a bow tie. Where have you been?"

"It's a secret," Brendan mumbled.

"And the dickie bow tie is supposed to make you look like James Bond?" said Mary, laughing. Brendan started to redden, and Mary wished she hadn't laughed. Brendan was always dangerous, particularly when drunk and angry.

"I've been on a mission near fucking Buckingham Palace." Brendan was very drunk. "With Chloe."

"Chloe?" Mary exclaimed. Mary was now concerned; she knew all about Chloe, who had been one of her housemates in the Ardoyne.

Mary had always suspected that Chloe was IRA, and she had never liked her that much. She was always hungry, raiding the fridge without contributing herself. She was also sly and nosy; more than once Mary had found her in her bedroom, supposedly just borrowing a comb or returning some nail varnish. But Mary guessed that Chloe could be very manipulative, and she probably had her brother under her thumb.

Mary's eyes looked down at the large bag on the kitchen floor, which she knew did not belong to her brother. She grabbed it without thinking and opened it on the kitchen table. Brendan made a half-hearted attempt to stop her, but his reactions were impaired by being so drunk. Mary took out some of the contents and spread them on the table; wires, timing devices and a pair of pliers. There were other items that Mary did not even recognise but she could tell that her brother was involved in making a bomb.

"Holy Jesus!" Mary gasped. "Is this a bomb?"

"None of your business!" Brendan started to put the various pieces of bomb-making equipment back in the bag, but he was so drunk that he dropped the pliers on the floor.

"Have you put a bomb in Buckingham Palace?" Mary's voice was incredulous.

"No, the other place by Green Park!"

Mary was shocked and struggled to understand what Brendan, with a bag of bomb-making equipment in her kitchen, was all about. She could tell it was bad news, and the revelation that St James' Palace – where she had been only hours earlier – was the target made the hair stand up on the back of her neck. But what to do? She was torn between protecting her brother and also saving her boyfriend of only two months from being killed in a bomb attack.

The decision was made for her when the front door opened and some of her housemates walked into the hallway. Mary wanted to be rid of Brendan before she had to explain his presence to her student friends. This was mainly for his own protection.

"Get out quickly before they see you!" Mary was shoving everything she could find back inside Brendan's bag. "Get out now," Mary hissed, in a whisper, and despite being only half as tall and heavy as her brother, she managed to bundle Brendan out onto the street. Fortunately, her housemates had gone straight upstairs after their night out, and she could hear them clattering around above the kitchen ceiling.

Mary found the remains of some whisky in a cupboard, then made her tea and poured the whisky into her cup. She needed to collect her thoughts quickly and before she was disturbed. She thought of ringing her mother at home in Strabane, but she didn't even have a telephone, and telephoning a neighbour would be complicated and likely to attract attention. She could talk it over with Sarah, but she didn't know when she would be back after supper with her mother. Moreover, talking to Sarah would not be easy; she would naturally take Colin's side and want to call the police as soon as possible.

She had to come up with a solution that would protect both her brother and her boyfriend. From the hall, she collected the small handbag that she had taken to St James'

Palace and took out her cigarettes. She lit up and started to think. Next to the cigarettes was a small slip of paper, which Colin had given her before going on guard duty. On the scrap of paper was a telephone number where Mary could reach Colin in the Officers' Mess in St James' Palace. Grabbing her coat, she went into the small hall, picked up some ten-pence pieces, and put them in her pocket. She was tempted to use the shared house phone in the hall, but she wanted privacy for what she had to do. She left the house quickly without telling any of her housemates where she was going, and she didn't want to explain herself. She was also anxious not to meet Sarah on her way back to the house because she would want to know where she was going, and she didn't want to lie to her friend. The red telephone box was in Shirland Mews, only a few minutes' walk away. Mary was irritated to see that the box was occupied by an elderly-looking woman who was in the midst of an earnest conversation that showed no sign of ending rapidly. As a result, while waiting, Mary used the time to practise what she had to say. She had always enjoyed mimicry and remembered teaching Colin the difference between how people spoke in the rural west of Northern Ireland and how they said things in Belfast. Eventually, the woman left the call box, and Mary entered gratefully. She put the pile of ten pence pieces on top of the telephone and rang the number. She was half expecting an operator, and she was a little startled when she heard Jeremy answer immediately. She shoved two ten-pence pieces into the slot as soon as she heard the pips.

Putting on her thickest and harshest Belfast accent, Mary demanded to speak to Colin, and then, when she was certain it was Colin on the line, she said, "There's a bomb. You get out now, Colin!"

As soon as she had finished, she walked, slowly this time, back to her house. She hoped she had done enough to warn Colin without harming Brendan. Suddenly she felt homesick and wanted to see her ailing mother back in Strabane and get away from London, and even from Colin, for a while. Her first set of exams were due at the end of the week, after which she had a week's holiday. If she could afford it, she would try to go home for a few days and spend some time with her mother.

Chapter Twenty-One

The whistle made a piercing shrill sound that went straight through Colin's head. He was instantly awake. It was still dark. He didn't know how long he had been allowed to sleep but it felt as if it was only a few minutes ago when he had collapsed exhausted on his bed after the night exercise.

"PT kit outside now!" an instructor known to Colin only as Brian shouted. Colin only took a few seconds to put on his PT kit which he had worn more in the last three weeks than ever before in the Army, including Sandhurst. He was glad he had a spare set as the kit he wore yesterday was still soaking wet after their long run through the forest that surrounded their camp. Once he was dressed, he ran out of the barrack hut to a small tarmac square that was the rallying point.

There were sixteen men left of the course and three women from the twenty-nine men and seven women who had started three weeks ago. They had been told that anyone could take themselves off the course at any time for whatever reason. All they had to do was to report to the Chief Instructor's office in the middle of the camp. Their accommodation was a simple barrack hut with a washroom and showers at one end. Each of them had a bed, in which they seldom slept, a wooden chair and a metal locker. The women were in a separate block on the other side of the rallying point which was out of bounds for the men and Colin suspected that the accommodation was no more comfortable for the girls than it was for the blokes.

The men were all present and ready for Brian to start his PT Session. Colin looked across to the women's block which the three girls had just left and were sprinting over to join them at the rallying point, pursued by one of the female instructors similar to a terrier chasing rabbits. Brian then gave the group a gruelling PT session which on this occasion involved another run into the forest with half of the group carrying large medicine balls, each one was the size of a beach ball but much heavier. The group had to share the load of the massive balls as they ran along a muddy track. After about an hour, Brian ended the PT session and told the group they could shower, change into combat clothing and get some breakfast.

Colin looked around the cookhouse as he ate his massive breakfast. All those on the course were there and eating voraciously. They were spread over six small tables with a larger table at one end of the room for the staff. None of those on the course dared sit with the instructors. There had been more tables at the start of the course but as those who remained were fewer by the day the number of tables had diminished. Meal times were the only opportunity for Colin to think about his situation.

This course was unlike anything he had encountered in the Army. There were no badges of rank and no surnames. At the start of the course, everyone was given a number that was used by the instructors and the students alike. It was made very clear at the outset that any attempt to enquire on someone's name or regiment would result in immediate failure and a return to your unit. In Colin's case, he was told that if he failed the course he would be returned to the not-so-tender custody of the Royal Military Police. Colin noticed that most of those on the course looked a few years older than him and were perhaps captains or even majors. He also suspected that some were from the Royal Navy or the RAF and perhaps civilians although, if they were, they would be tough to survive the rigorous training.

There was one face that Colin did recognise. Captain Sarah Matthews of the Royal Military Police was one of the instructors and was having her breakfast on the table reserved for their use. But she wore nothing to indicate her rank or her unit. She was known on the course simply as Jenny and Colin wondered if she really was part of the Military Police. This morning she was sitting next to another pretty female instructor called Annie and was deep in conversation. Sarah, or Jenny, looked up suddenly and caught Colin's eye for a moment and Colin wondered if he was the subject of their earnest talk.

There was no course programme. Interspersed with the PT there were other tests, all without warning. Yesterday, Colin was told to walk into a room in one of the camp huts to collect some glasses and bring them back to where they were about to hear a lecture. As soon as he returned, he was told to write down everything he had seen in the room where he had spent no more than ten seconds.

Suddenly the whistle shrilled again, and Colin was brought back to the present. "Everyone in the lecture hall now!" shouted Brian. Colin rushed out of the cookhouse and ran to the lecture hall. He had no idea what was going to happen next.

Colin was both wrong and right about Sarah Matthews. He was wrong to doubt her real identity. Sarah Matthews was her real name, and she served as a captain in the Royal Military Police. She had already done a tour with the Detachment in Northern Ireland and was now one of the instructors on the course. At the same time, Colin was right to think that he had been the subject of their conversation. This conversation continued after breakfast in the Chief Instructor's office. While Colin and the other students were attending a lecture on Close Target Reconnaissance, or CTR, Sarah and the other instructors were deciding who should stay on the course and who should be sent back to their units.

Immediately after their lecture, Colin and the others were told to grab a groundsheet and an extra jumper. They were then grouped in pairs and shown on the map a target that they had to recce. They were bundled on the back of a four-ton truck and driven into the forest, with each pair dropping off along the way. Colin was paired with Number 47, a short, wiry man who looked about five years his senior. From his accent, Colin guessed that he came from

Liverpool. When it was their turn, an instructor checked that they knew where they were on the map and then gave them the grid reference of the target, which was about five kilometres away. They were told to move to the target as quickly as possible and, without being observed, mount a covert observation post. Colin and his Liverpudlian friend set off into the forest, heading for the target. They were both so fit after three weeks on the course that they reached their objective very quickly and set about finding a suitable place from where to watch the target – a small bridge over a stream next to a narrow lane. They found a thick bush surrounded by stinging nettles, and, lying on their stomachs, they crawled into the centre of the bush from where they could observe the bridge. It was very cold and looked like it was going to rain. Their equipment did little to protect them from the cold, and they had no idea how long they had to maintain their watch. Nothing was happening on the bridge, and by nightfall, the situation was unchanged, except for the fact that both watchers were now freezing and very hungry.

The next morning, they heard a very faint rustling sound behind them, and one of the instructors was crawling into their hiding place. With a shrug, he gave them both a slice of white bread and a sip of water from a bottle, told them to continue their watch and crawled away. A few hours after he left, a white van stopped on the bridge for a few minutes and then drove off. Without binoculars, it was impossible to read the registration number or see who was driving the van. This icy vigil continued for several hours. Both Colin and 47 were wet through by now despite the meagre protection offered by the groundsheet. And then, without warning, the instructor returned and, pointing to his white armband to indicate authority, he told them both to run down to the road with their equipment. As they reached the lane, they were joined by other pairs from the course who also looked very tired and cold. After a few minutes, there were roughly nineteen present and the instructor told them all to form three ranks before, he said, a run back to camp. This news sent morale plummeting, as it was at least ten miles to camp and everyone was exhausted. Nevertheless, the group set off on a slow jog. Everyone had stiff joints and, at first, it was very difficult to run, but gradually the pace quickened. For three men and one woman, this was too much, and they collapsed on the side of the lane, exercising their right to leave the course. After about a mile, they ran past a steep bend where a four-ton truck was parked, and they were told to climb inside. Colin realised that it was never the plan for everyone to run back to camp; the instructors just wanted to identify those who were sufficiently determined to attempt it.

Back at camp, they clambered off the truck's back. There were only a handful left after the observation exercise and the run that followed, during which several on the course had dropped out and would soon be returning to their units. Those that remained were told to enter a nondescript barracks hut, which no one had entered before. Once inside, they were met by a group of instructors who made them all put on blindfolds. Sarah Matthews, or Jenny, as she was called on the course, fastened Colin's blindfold, smiling as she did so. Colin had no idea what, if anything, was funny but he guessed he would soon find out. Once they were all blindfolded, they heard a door opening and they were all shepherded through, after which they heard the door slam shut.

After a few moments, a loud voice shouted. "Take your blindfolds off!"

Colin reached up to his head, removed his blindfold and opened his eyes. It was pitch dark and he couldn't see anything, not even his own hands. He had no idea if anyone was in the room with him. Suddenly, very bright lights came on, and Colin and the others found themselves in a large gym, in the centre of which was a boxing ring. In the middle of the boxing ring, the chief instructor stood alone, holding a notice board. He then announced that they were all going to do some milling. Colin had heard of milling but had never experienced it before. The Chief Instructor took a few moments to explain the few rules that existed. In pairs, they would enter the ring wearing boxing gloves and then, for a timed three minutes, try and knock the living daylights out of their partner. Colin was still paired with Number 47 from Liverpool, who had not given up on the run and was still on the course. Colin noted that he was a few inches taller than Number 47, encouraging him to think that this would help him in the ring even without boxing experience. But Colin was wrong. Much later, Colin learned that his milling partner had boxed for the Army, and Colin left the boxing ring badly bruised.

The next morning, those that were still on the course were told to go to the lecture hall, where Jenny took control. She said that the following should report to the Chief Instructor immediately and then read out the names of roughly half of those in the hall. When they had left, Colin expected to be told that they had all failed and would be leaving the course. Instead, though, Jenny told them that they had passed the initial selection and would be continuing their training after a short weekend break. Colin looked round the room and was pleased to see that Number 47 was still on the course. They exchanged rueful grins, and Colin noticed that he had a small bruise over his left eye. *Perhaps I did manage to land a blow on him after all,* he thought. They started to leave the hall to get ready for their break when Jenny called him over. Colin was alarmed to see that Sergeant Hansen had joined her. Colin had not seen the sergeant since the helicopter flight from the Duke of York barracks.

"Sorry, Colin, no weekend leave for you. You've got to stay here."

Chapter Twenty-Two

The Regimental Adjutant glanced at the two files on his tray. He would have preferred to look outside his window onto the drill square in Wellington Barracks and Birdcage Walk beyond. He could hear band music playing in the forecourt of Buckingham Palace as the Queen's Guard was changing. The old guard would be marching back into Wellington Barracks in about twenty minutes, and he wanted to watch the dismount to make sure that the drill and turnout were of the highest standard.

With a sigh, he turned to the two files sitting in his in-tray, which were the only pieces of work outstanding. His desk was exceptionally tidy; only a regimental diary, a fountain pen and a calendar lay beside his tray. The first of two files, both of which had a blue cover, had the name I F Munro typed neatly on the front. Captain Munro had just been selected to be the ADC for Major General Smythe, the newly appointed Commander of Security Forces Northern Ireland. General Smythe was a Guards officer and had served in the regiment with distinction leading to staff college, command of the regiment, a brigadier's appointment and now a very senior role in Northern Ireland. It was the convention that a major general in command should be accompanied by an aide de camp, or

ADC, normally chosen from the general's original regiment. He reviewed Munro's file quickly: did well at Sandhurst, appears to be a good soldier, efficient, etc. But something was missing; none of his reports showed any warmth for the man, and the Regimental Adjutant wondered how much he was liked by his fellow officers. Of course, his brother officers had enjoyed invitations to shoot and fish on his estate in Perthshire, but this all sounded a little contrived. He wondered why the file had been brought to his attention today and saw with alarm that Munro needed to be positively vetted for his role as an ADC; he would see some very secret documents working for the CSF.

This irritated the Regimental Adjutant; PV clearance should have been obtained before Munro started the job, not when he was already in post. *Oh well,* he thought, *better get the security people on the job as soon as possible.*

He knew there was very little he could do about the second blue file with the name C Smith on the cover. He wanted to know what was going on with Colin Smith since his abrupt departure from Chelsea Barracks at the hands of the military police. No one knew where he was, and the military police weren't talking. He had heard a rumour that special forces or intelligence services may be involved, but nothing was being said, and the Regimental Adjutant needed to know when, or if ever, he would be returning to the regiment. Only last week, on the pretext of visiting a friend at the MOD, the Regimental Adjutant wandered into the office of someone he believed had been in special forces and asked him casually if he knew anything about Colin Smith. When he returned to his office in Birdcage Walk twenty minutes later, he found his chief clerk waiting for him and looking very anxious. Apparently, the brigade major had telephoned and wanted to see the Regimental Adjutant immediately. He quickly checked his turnout and rushed over to horse guards and asked for the brigade major. In the event, it was not the brigade major but the Major General himself who saw him in his office and then proceeded to give him the grilling of his life and threatened an immediate sacking if he ever asked questions again about things 'that did not concern him'. It was a little unfair to suggest Colin Smith did not concern him as his postings – both inside and outside the regiment – were very much his affair but, in the circumstances, he did not dare mention this to the Major General.

The Regimental Adjutant sat down behind his desk, and reluctantly, he skimmed through Colin's file. It made for interesting reading; he was the only grammar-school-educated officer in the regiment. He had left Reading Grammar School with three excellent A Levels and had been offered a place at Oxford, but he had decided to join the Army instead. Under 'Interests', where most of his brother officers would list field sports such as hunting or shooting, Colin had written rally racing and rock climbing. He noted that his maternal grandmother was German, and the file said he spoke the language fluently. *Not that it will do you much good wherever you are now,* he thought with a grim smile. He wondered why he had joined the Guards; he was much more suited to a line infantry regiment, but then he checked his glowing reports from Sandhurst, where he met and became a close friend of Johnny Keynsham. The two were now inseparable. Most of the officers seemed to like Colin Smith, the exceptions being Iain Munro and Jeremy Kershaw. Of course, it helped that Colin was a good soldier, and Jeremy Kershaw had to respect him as a result. On the back of the file was the commendation for being mentioned in dispatches during the Belfast tour. Colin did not realise that Jeremy Kershaw had initially recommended Colin for this award.

Chapter Twenty-Three

Colin complained bitterly about not being allowed out of camp for a short break like the rest of those still on the course, but to no avail. To reinforce the point, he was hauled into yet another small office, where he was confronted by none other than the so-called Major Smith, this time in civilian clothes, looking very dapper in a dark suit and tie.

"Resigned your commission, Major?" asked Colin flippantly. "Or have you just run out of different uniforms to wear?"

"Oh, shut up," Major Smith replied testily, and laid three photographs on a small table in the middle of the office. "Tell me what you know about these three."

Colin looked down and saw three faces staring up at him. One was a very tough-looking, broad-set man with a grim and determined expression; next to him was a smaller man who looked less aggressive. But the two faces looked similar – perhaps brothers. The third photo sent a cold shiver down his spine as he looked down at a picture of his girlfriend, Mary.

"Nothing to say, Colin? Gone quiet all of a sudden," said Major Smith.

"Why have you got a picture of my girlfriend?" asked Colin crossly.

"Calm down," Major Smith replied. "Precisely because she is your girlfriend and because of her two brothers. Remember that gunfight in Colinward Street?"

Colin nodded.

"We believe these two, Mary Flynn's brothers, were the ones who shot at you. We also believe through our sources in the South that this one, Pat, received emergency surgery for a gunshot wound. He will walk with a limp for the rest of his life. You were the only one to return fire that night. That means you were the one to put a bullet into Pat Flynn."

"Brendan is the tougher of the two," Major Smith continued. If he finds out that a Brit is having it off with his sister, and that the same Brit nearly killed his brother, he'll stop at nothing to kill you."

"They can't possibly make the connection to me, can they?" Colin queried.

"Don't be so sure. The IRA has their sources as well as ours. So you're here as much for your own protection as keeping the military police happy, who would lock you up if you as much as set foot out of the camp."

Given the unyielding nature of his interview with Major Smith and Sarah Matthews, Colin was very surprised to hear that he was at least allowed to telephone home. There was a call box in the mess, which he was told to use, and he was told to be very careful about what he could and could not say. He was told to say nothing about

Mary Flynn. After initially feeling pleased that he could telephone, his heart sank when he realised that Sarah Matthews would be standing beside him when he made the call. His one permitted call was to his home in Reading and Colin hoped that someone would be there to answer. Thankfully, after four rings, his mother answered, who was thrilled to hear his voice but also clearly worried about her son. It turned out that Jeremy Kershaw, of all people, had contacted her. Jeremy had told her that Colin was on an 'Adventure Training Course' in Wales and was doing well. Surprisingly, no further mention had been made of the military police. After an awkward conversation, with Sarah Matthews listening carefully, his mother passed the handset to his sister. Colin found it easier talking to his sister, and she sounded in good spirits and full of enthusiasm about a career in medicine. Colin wanted to ask her about Mary, but he couldn't do so with Sarah Matthews standing a few feet away. Fortunately, his sister offered the information anyway: Mary had left London for Northern Ireland because her mother was very ill. Colin would have liked to ask whether she had Mary's address or telephone number, but that was not possible.

Colin spent a miserable weekend at the camp, but at least he was allowed to catch up on some sleep. He was given a room to himself in what was apparently the Instructors' Mess that would normally be out of bounds while the course was in progress. The camp was nearly deserted apart from a skeleton crew guarding the camp, but at least he was warm and could relax. The cookhouse was manned, and his appetite was as healthy as ever, so Colin spent the time either sleeping or eating. The not-very talkative Sergeant Hansen RMP also spent the weekend on camp, and, although nothing was said, Colin guessed that his presence was to deter him from making a run.

After the short weekend, the course resumed with renewed intensity. They were kept very busy and under pressure at all times. But there was also a new purpose to the course, and Colin soon realised that what he was now being taught would soon have to be put into practice in a hostile area. There was a lot of firearms training and live firing on the ranges, starting with the Browning 9mm pistol that Colin had fired a few times since arriving at Sandhurst. In one day on the course, he fired more 9mm rounds than he had fired in his life previously. Then they moved on to other weapons that were new to Colin, including small machine pistols that could be hidden under a jacket. As well as firing weapons of all shapes and sizes, much of their time was spent on a combination of surveillance techniques and driver training. At first, they would mount fairly simple exercises, such as following a man or woman, known as a target, on foot in the local town. Then these exercises became more advanced, with the target being a suspect vehicle that was followed by several cars all in radio contact with each other.

Surveillance from cars required advanced levels of driving skill, often at speed. It had been made clear that this was something everyone had to master if they wanted to pass the course. One cold morning, Colin and Number 47 were on the firing range when Jenny appeared and told them to get into her car, which was parked nearby. Number

47 was in the front passenger seat while Colin was told to take a backseat. Jenny then proceeded to demonstrate the speed and skill required of a driver when driving in a hostile area. After a bit of banter about women drivers, Jenny drove off at speed. Colin was impressed; she drove fast, but she always seemed to be in control and was able to pass other vehicles quickly and safely while giving them both a running commentary on how she was driving and why. After about twenty minutes, Jenny pulled to the side of the road by a small barn, where she explained that they were five miles away from camp via small country roads and lanes. By the end of the course, everyone had to pass the speed test, which was simply to reach camp as quickly as possible without harming members of the public. Jenny did not say what was regarded as a good time but told Number 47 to time her and she set off. Less than four minutes later, after a series of high-speed corners and overtaking a tractor, their car pulled in by the entrance to the camp. Colin had to agree it was impressive driving, while Number 47 looked a little pale. It was the turn of Number 47 to take the wheel, and off he set cautiously at first. He found overtaking at speed difficult and responded by driving far too slowly for most of the session. But Jenny encouraged him, and after a while, he started to drive quicker and better. However, his timed speed test was a poor six minutes, and Jenny said he would have to improve if he wanted to pass the course.

It was Colin's turn. From the start, he found driving the car easy, and he barely needed Jenny's instructions on how to overtake and corner effectively. When it came to his speed test, it was Colin's dream – he forgot he was on the course but was back on a rally circuit. At one point, when overtaking a lorry through a gap that barely existed, he thought he sensed even Jenny flinching. When he pulled in at the camp, Jenny, slightly short of breath, admitted, "That was... that was very fast!" Number 47 staggered out of the back seat and was violently sick in front of the camp gates.

The tough guy stuff was taught by members of the SAS, whose base at Hereford was nearby. Again, no ranks or uniforms were involved, and the instructors simply introduced themselves by their first names, which might or might not have been genuine. There was a studied casualness in their teaching style.

"Right, my name is Wayne, and today I'm going to show you what to do if you're unarmed and someone points a gun at you. First thing to say is that if you ever find yourself in this position, you've fucked up big time. You'll always be armed, and yesterday Kev told you how to hit someone hard enough to give you time to draw your weapon." Wayne then told Colin to stand opposite him. Even though there were no ranks on the course, everyone knew that Colin was an officer, and the instructors enjoyed demonstrating new techniques on officers before anyone else.

"Right, boss," Wayne ordered. "Hit me like Kev said and draw your weapon!" Colin managed to strike a weak blow with the palm of his hand to Wayne's chest, but he only touched his shoulder holster before he took a heavy blow from Wayne in return.

"You got to be quicker than that, boss." Wayne chuckled. "Everyone, get in your pairs and practise what Kev said."

Colin found himself with Number 47 as his sparring partner. However, by this stage of the course, the requirement to call everyone by a number had been dropped, and first names were being used instead. So, Barry was now Number 47, and Barry knew how to strike a hard blow. Colin and Barry swapped roles; at first, Barry would try and hit Colin to give himself time to draw his weapon, while Colin would try and land a blow to stop him. Then Colin would try and draw his weapon quickly, and so on for about thirty minutes, after which Wayne told everyone to stop and listen in. The next item was, as promised, disarming someone pointing a gun at you. This was a high-risk action that involved grabbing hold of the weapon in your left hand while turning your whole body to the right at the same time.

"What do you do if the person pointing the gun at you is out of touching distance?" Colin asked.

"You've fucked up even worse," Wayne replied.

"What about distracting your enemy?" Colin persisted.

"How're you going to do that? You're unarmed, and an IRA gunman is pointing a pistol at you."

"Your flies are undone," said Colin, who noticed that Wayne's eyes dropped for a fraction.

"Oh, very fucking funny, boss, but if that's how you hope to survive in Ireland, fucking good luck."

Chapter Twenty-Four

There were twelve people left on the course: ten men and two women. None of them realised that it was their last day, even when they were all ordered to gather in the lecture hall and the chief instructor stood on the small stage at one end of the room.

"The following people are to go and wait outside my office," he said.

Then Colin realised this was when they would hear whether they had passed or failed the course. Colin hoped he would not hear his name. Without pausing, the chief instructor read out six names that included both Colin and Barry. The six of them, which included one girl, left the lecture hall, trying to avoid eye contact with those who were still seated, and made their way over to the chief's office. They didn't have long to wait until the chief arrived and summoned all of them into his office. Colin noticed that he looked a little ruffled.

"Right, shut the door. You lot have all passed. The other lot in the lecture hall didn't make it and will be leaving us immediately. I never like giving bad news. You're all to stay here until they've left the camp." The chief almost looked upset.

"Some of you will be taking a short period of leave. Not you, Colin and Barry; you're both flying to Belfast tonight."

Chapter Twenty-Five

Captain Iain Munro, Aide de Camp to Major General Sir Jocelyn Smythe Bt, the newly appointed Director of Security Forces Northern Ireland, was feeling very smug as he sat in his small office outside the much larger office for the general. From his window, he could look west across the River Foyle and the city of Londonderry beyond. The Director of Security Forces (NI) was a newly created post as it was felt that another two-star officer was needed in the province. Moreover, it had been decided that the general's headquarters should be in the west of the province, as opposed to Headquarters Northern Ireland in Lisburn, where there were already two generals. As a result, General Sir Jocelyn's headquarters was in Ebrington Barracks, just a few yards away from the headquarters for the 7th Infantry Brigade. Needless to say, the brigade commander did not particularly enjoy having a two-star general so close to his headquarters. The situation was made much worse by the fact that these two senior officers did not like each other. Brigadier Ian Jones had been commissioned into the Royal Anglian Regiment and had often found Guards officers to be arrogant towards the line infantry. Unfortunately for Ian Jones, when he attended the staff college at Camberley, he had Smythe as his director, and the two disliked each other on site. The ill feeling that existed between the two commanders trickled down to their respective staffs, and the two formations did not communicate with each other as well as they should. From Munro's perspective, he found the friction between the two senior commanders and their staffs highly entertaining, especially as he hated the whole lot of them anyway. The situation also gave him plenty of opportunity to be unpleasant, which he enjoyed immensely. Acting on his general's behalf, he was able to tell the brigade's staff officers what was required in advance of a formal visit. If he had been a helpful and considerate officer, he would have given the staff some warning about the general's plans and his requirements. However, Munro was neither helpful nor considerate, except when it served his interests to do so, and he liked to spring news of what the general wanted on the staff officers at the last possible moment.

At first, Munro could not believe the amount of classified information he was privy to in his role as the general's ADC. He was copied into most of the confidential and secret documents that crossed the general's desk, which usually included details of forthcoming operations against the IRA. However, Munro gained the most valuable information by accompanying the general on his trips around the province. He had visited most of the key operational bases in Northern Ireland, including RUC Springfield Road, Creggan Camp and Crossmaglen, where he learned about patrolling reports and the Army's intelligence assessment of the IRA.

Since starting as the general's ADC, Munro's biggest problem had been how to pass on secret information to the IRA. To help him, Ciaran had inserted a low-level agent in Ebrington barracks, employed as a waiter in the Officers' Mess. It was a very busy mess, servicing staff officers from the two headquarters and the infantry battalion based in the barracks. The Army had no alternative but to employ local civilians to keep both the Officers' Mess and Sergeants' Mess running smoothly. All civilians had to be vetted but this was rudimentary. Ciaran's agent had no clue about Munro's identity, and Munro knew nothing about the agent, nor did he want to.

Munro glanced at his watch, an expensive Rolex and more practical than his fob watch, which he wore in Chelsea Barracks. He had time for lunch in the Officers' Mess before his briefing for the general at two p.m. to review the arrangements for his dinner party that evening. He picked up his forage cap, checked himself in the mirror outside his office, and told the general's secretary that he would be out for an hour. The general's secretary was an efficient civil servant from Manchester, and she was glad to have an hour to herself before Munro's return.

The Officers' Mess in Ebrington Barracks was an imposing building on a hill looking west over the River Foyle. Munro walked across the square and up a steep flight of steps to the front entrance of the mess. He pushed open the large wooden door and walked past the dining room on his left and the TV room on his right. He found himself in a tall-ceilinged hall, where he turned right into the corridor leading towards the bar on the left. Just before turning into the bar, there was a notice board where the President of the Mess Committee would publish details of forthcoming events and functions, such as the Curry Lunch to be held at 1300 hours on the third Sunday of every month. It also displayed terse minutes from the PMC reminding everyone that their mess bills should be paid promptly. The PMC was a major in the infantry battalion based in Ebrington Barracks and had an eye for detail, with the notice board reflecting the tight control he kept on the mess. Every notice had one brass drawing pin in each corner, and the notices were all laid out in straight lines, rather like a company of guardsmen on a parade ground. Around the notice board was a plain wooden edge. As Munro turned left into the bar, he was relieved to see one green drawing pin in the wooden edge at the top right corner of the notice board. Earlier the same day, Munro had placed a blue drawing pin in the same place, meaning let's meet next Tuesday. The green drawing pin meant that Munro's message had been received and would be passed on.

Kevin Doherty had been very glad to be offered the job in the Officers' Mess in Ebrington barracks. There wasn't much work for a fifty-year-old in Derry, and when he heard that the Brits wanted waiters and kitchen staff, he decided to apply. Fortunately for Kevin, a stint as a barman on a ferry a few years earlier had helped him get the position of 'waiter' in the Officers' Mess. Initially, he was anxious that the Provos would disapprove of him working for the Brits, and he mentioned this when he next met a friend in McCain's bar who he suspected might be working for the IRA. To his surprise, he was told to take the job, keep his eyes and ears open, and be ready to help if asked. Refusing to comply with these simple instructions was not a serious option for Kevin if he wanted to avoid a bullet in his left kneecap.

Only a week after starting the job, again, while drinking in McCain's bar, his friend told him about the noticeboard outside the bar in the mess. He was told about the coloured drawing pin that would sometimes appear on the side of the noticeboard, and, carrying a duster so that he could say he was dusting the wooden edge, he should remove the pin and replace it with a green drawing pin from his stock of pins that his friend in McCains had provided. Then, when he finished his shift, he would ring a number from a callbox in McCains, ask for Martin, and reveal the colour of the drawing pin. Kevin was told that under no circumstances should he loiter near the notice board or attempt to spot who was planting drawing pins on the side of the notice board.

As for Munro, he had no interest in knowing who was removing his pin and replacing it with a green one. The important thing for Munro was that a green pin meant his message had been received and passed on. The other problem that had exercised Munro and Ciaran was where they should meet. Munro was kept very busy by his general and could not wander off at short notice to meet Ciaran or anyone else. Although the immediate area around Ebrington Barracks was Protestant territory and relatively safe for off-duty soldiers in plain clothes, the policy was to keep such trips outside the barracks to a minimum and travel in pairs. The game of golf offered a solution for Ciaran and Munro. Eight miles to the east of Londonderry was Eglington Golf Course, just north of the Limavady Road. Army officers were allowed to play there occasionally, as it was considered safe enough. Munro had learnt to play in Scotland, and when he discovered that one of the Brigade staff officers was a keen player, they arranged a nine-hole round at Eglington once a fortnight that took only a couple of hours, enough time for a game without being out of the headquarters for too long. Munro was much the better of the two players, much to the irritation of the young staff officer, who did wonder why, always on the fifth hole, Munro sliced his ball to the right, where it landed in some trees that were difficult to see clearly from the fairway.

"Drat! I've sliced it to the right again. You take your shot!" Munro would say. "I'll go and find my ball." It would have been better manners to stay and watch his opponent play his shot, but Munro didn't care about manners and he walked off rapidly to the trees, ostensibly to find his golf ball but, more importantly, to drop a package in the rough a few feet away from where he could see Ciaran, golf club in hand, who was busy searching for the ball that he had played from another fairway.

After buying a tonic water, Munro turned right out of the bar, noted the green drawing pin out of the corner of his eye, and went straight to the dining room, where lunch was now being served. He spoke to no one during the meal because he was deeply concerned about what he should report next Tuesday and how he could gather the information without raising suspicion. After his lunch, he didn't linger in the mess to read the newspapers or share a coffee with another officer, but went straight back to his office to prepare himself for his two p.m. meeting with the general and, more importantly, as far as Munro was concerned, prepare himself for his meeting with Ciaran next Tuesday.

Munro knew he could not pass on everything he knew from within the headquarters of the Director of Security Forces (NI), and he had to be selective. His meetings with Ciaran were little more than a brush pass, with small packages being exchanged under the cover of searching for a golf ball in the rough. He might have the chance to whisper a few words to Ciaran, but this could not be guaranteed. Munro decided to focus on what he knew about new activity in the three villages of Claudy, Feeny and Park, which formed a triangle in rural Co Derry, about twenty miles south-east of Ebrington Barracks. He had seen the general and his chief of staff studying a map of the area only yesterday.

The telephone rang sharply on Munro's desk.

"ADC," said Munro into the handset.

"Please may I speak to Captain Iain Munro?" The voice was English, polite but official.

"This is Captain Munro speaking," Munro replied, for some reason feeling slightly uneasy.

"My name's John Reynolds; I'm with the MOD Vetting Service, and I need to have an interview with you."

Munro felt his pulse rate quicken. "Yes, I see. Well, we're very busy this week, but maybe one day later this month?"

"I really need to see you right away. You see, you should have had your PV clearance before starting your current job. I've just spoken to your general, and he tells me he can spare you for a couple of hours at four p.m. today, so I'll come to your office then. Bye for now."

Munro slumped onto his chair. He felt anxious and deflated. "And just when things were going so well!"

After a few moments, he opened his top right drawer and found a small plastic tub of drawing pins, from which he took out two red pins, the signal for an emergency meeting.

Chapter Twenty-Six

Mary had only intended to stay with her mother for a few days. After telephoning the bomb warning, Mary wanted time to get away and settle her thoughts. There was plenty to think over; she was falling in love with Colin, but he was a British officer, for pity's sake! Then there were her two brothers, Pat and Brendan, who were probably both IRA. Brendan was particularly dangerous and was almost literally a walking time bomb. To make matters even more complicated, she was really enjoying her course at Imperial and felt she was doing well, while at the same time making new friends, especially Colin's sister, Sarah.

But she only had to take one look at her mother to realise that she needed to be closer. After the long bus journey from Aldergrove Airport to Strabane, Mary was sad to see that her mother was not there to meet her at the bus station. In the past, she had always met Mary after she had been away, and then they would walk together from the town centre to their home in the Ballycolman. But on this occasion, Mary made the familiar journey by herself, past the Brit checkpoint on Bridge Street, over the Mourne River, and into the Ballycolman Estate. It was not far, and Mary only had a small bag to carry, not expecting to stay long with her mother. She had a key to the front door, which she opened, and the first thing that Mary noticed was the strong smell of cigarettes. Her mother had always been a heavy smoker, and Mary had hoped that she might have cut down, but this was clearly not happening. Mary called out a brief hello, to which there was no response, and walked into the sitting room to find her mother sprawled on a sofa. She appeared to be conscious, but only just, and Mary suspected she had spent the night on the sofa after a night of drinking. An empty bottle that had probably contained potcheen lay on its side on the sofa, surrounded by empty cigarette packets. Mary guessed that the supplier of the illicit drink had also smuggled the cheap cigarettes over the border.

"Come on, Ma!" said Mary as she tried to shake her mother awake, first gently and then with more vigour.

"It's lovely to see you, Mary, dear. What brings you home?"

"I said I was coming home for a few days, Ma." Mary spoke with a sigh, depressed that her mother had apparently completely forgotten about her visit.

It took her the next twenty-four hours to sort things out for her mother. The house was dirty and untidy, with unwashed dishes stacked up in the kitchen sink. The fridge contained little that was safe to eat and most of its contents had to go straight to the bin. After cooking her mother a simple lunch, Mary persuaded her, with some difficulty, to take a bath, change into a clean set of clothes and have a rest. Meanwhile, Mary set about cleaning the house and buying in some provisions to restock the fridge.

As she worked, Mary became angry. Where were her useless two brothers, Brendan and Pat? They were supposed to be looking after Ma. Mary spoke to the neighbours in the street, one of whom Bernadette, Mary had known since she was a girl, but Bernadette's reports were not encouraging. Neither Brendan nor Pat visited their mother regularly but would turn up occasionally late at night, often with others who Bernadette did not recognise. Then, after a drinking session, they would leave and disappear again for weeks. Mary suspected that her brothers were the ones who delivered the illegal potcheen and the fags, this being the extent to which they were prepared to help their mother.

The next few days were very busy for Mary. Once she realised she would have to stay in Northern Ireland, there were several difficult decisions to make. Imperial was at the top of the list, and she managed to persuade the college to let her miss the remainder of this year's course in order to restart the course next year. It helped that Mary's performance to date had been very strong. Mary found it very hard to delay her medical training; it had meant so much to her, and by postponing her studies, she felt that life in Northern Ireland was beginning to suffocate her. Although she needed to be nearer to her mother, Mary also needed to earn some money. Apart from meagre benefits, her mother had no income, her two brothers were unemployed, and, even when they had any money, it went on drink. Mary tried to find a nursing job locally, but Strabane had the highest level of unemployment in

Europe, and all the nursing jobs were filled. When she first returned to Northern Ireland, she had been in touch with Sister Kath, and they had agreed to meet when they both had the chance. As a result, Mary asked Bernadette to look after her mother for the day while Mary took the bus to Belfast to see Sister Kath on her day off. When Mary brought her up to date with her life, Kath immediately wanted to help and said that she would have a few words at the RVH. When Mary returned to Strabane, she felt heartened by her chat with Kath but did not expect to hear from her. However, Mary had forgotten the extent of Sister Kath's influence within the RVH, and a few days later, their neighbour Bernadette, who had a functioning telephone in her house, called across the garden to say that Mary had a call from Belfast. Kath had arranged for Mary to resume nursing at the RVH on a part-time basis. Mary would work Monday through Thursday lunchtimes, returning to Strabane on Thursday afternoons. Bernadette said she would keep an eye on Mary's mother on the days that Mary would be in Belfast, making sure she ate regularly. In return, Mary would pay her a little of her badly needed nursing salary. The plan worked well. Mary's mother benefited from the regular attention and Mary enjoyed nursing again, even if it was not training to be a doctor.

One afternoon, after finishing her shift at the RVH, she walked back to the house on Crocus Street that she shared with Sister Kath. She and Kath had become very good friends since her return to Northern Ireland, and

Mary had gladly accepted her kind offer to rent a room in her house for a very small sum. As soon as she opened the front door, she knew that something was wrong.

"Mary, dear, it's your brothers Brendan and Pat!"

Mary's heart stopped. "Oh, God! Have the Brits shot them?"

"No, but they've been arrested and taken to the police base on Springfield Road."

"I must go and see them." Mary reached for her coat, which she had only just taken off.

"I'll come with you," Kath replied. Mary was about to say there was no need, but in truth, she would be glad of moral support when entering the base that the police shared with the Brits.

RUC Springfield Road was located at the eastern end of Springfield Road, very close to where it forms a crossroads with Falls Road and Grosvenor Road. It was a large, sinister-looking building heavily protected by sangars and high fencing, with armed Brits manning the perimeter. Everyone knew it was the main base in West Belfast for both the RUC and the British Army, and if you were Roman Catholic, it was somewhere to avoid. Nurse Donovan had once told her that if she was walking along Springfield Road, she even crossed to the other side of the road when passing the base. So it was that Mary, with Sister Kath in support, both in their nurses' uniforms, walked the short distance from Crocus Street to RUC Springfield Road. At the front entrance, a British soldier peered out of a guard post and asked them what they wanted.

"My name is Mary Flynn. I've come to see Inspector Irvine." Sister Kath had been given Irving's name earlier.

"Wait there," came the reply, and the sentry disappeared from view. About two minutes later, another face appeared – an officer this time – who said that Inspector Irvine was not available and that they should report back the next morning.

Sister Kath went on the attack immediately. "Now look you's here, young man! This poor wee girl is worried sick about her two brothers who are being interrogated in your dungeons as we speak. She needs to see them, nahh."

"Please wait a moment." The officer, looking a little pale, appeared to be changing his mind.

"Well, hurry up, young man. This poor girl has just come off her shift nursing the wounded after RUC brutality, and you are keeping her out here in the cold!"

It was actually quite a warm day, but Mary shivered anyway to show support for Sister Kath.

Another officer appeared who looked worried and anxious to do the right thing. The two nurses in their RVH uniforms were an impressive sight standing outside the gates on Springfield Road, and the noisy one could easily cause trouble. It would take very little to turn an argument with the two nurses into a full-blown riot.

Fortunately for the officer, Inspector Irvine suddenly appeared and acknowledged that he had left a message for Mary Flynn about her two brothers, who were being questioned inside. The sentry opened the gate, and the two nurses were summoned inside, which reminded Mary of a cowboy base in a western; a very tall fence formed a square with a sentry post in each corner. But this fence was made of sheet metal, unlike the wooden forts seen in the movies.

There was a car park where a mixture of army and police land rovers were parked up, all facing outwards. Both Mary and Kath were ushered inside the main building, which was just as ugly up close as it looked from Springfield Road. However, they were glad not to be taken downstairs but up two flights of stairs to a long corridor with chairs and benches along one side and doors presumably leading to offices on the other. They were both asked to sit down. After only a couple of minutes, Inspector Irvine, wearing the uniform of an inspector in the RUC, spoke to them both.

"Mary Flynn, come in here, please."

Kath rose to her feet together with Mary.

"Just Miss Flynn, if you please," said Inspector Irvine firmly.

"It's all right, Kath, I'll be OK," said Mary as she followed the inspector into the small, dingy office consisting of only a wooden table with two chairs facing each other.

"Sit down, please," said the inspector. He was a tall man who Mary guessed to be in his forties, with brown hair and flecks of grey and he was overweight. In fact, his RUC uniform worked hard to keep his large stomach buttoned up. He sat down with a grateful sigh and started to speak.

"Thank you for coming in to see us, Miss Flynn." He was being polite, almost gentle. "First of all, I have some good news. Your two brothers, Brendan and Pat, are free to go; we just had a few questions for them. They'll be up here in a minute."

The inspector then proceeded to ask Mary a set of mundane questions; full names, date of birth, place of work and current address. While this went on, another man entered the room from a door behind the inspector's chair and stood with his back to the wall without saying a word.

Mary soon became impatient. "Look, Inspector, you know the answer to all these questions already. I'm from Strabane, where I try to look after my mother. For pity's sake, I work part-time at the RVH to earn some cash. "Now, can I see my brothers or not?"

"Yes, of course, Miss Flynn. Just wait here, please, while I see what's happening."

Inspector Flynn left the small office, leaving Mary alone in the room with the grey-haired man, who had not yet spoken a word. He just stood there in a suit, looking at her.

"Who are you then, Mister?" Mary asked sharply.

"My name is Major Smith. I'm a friend – well, more of a colleague – of your boyfriend, another Smith, Colin Smith."

"Colin? You know Colin? Where is he?" Mary asked anxiously.

"Oh, he's been busy. Sends you his love, of course."

"But is he all right?"

"Oh, he'll be fine. You only have a moment before your two brothers arrive. Here's a telephone number; if you want to help him again, ring this and ask for Major Smith." At this point, Major Smith left a slip of paper on the desk and left the room. Seconds later, the door opened and in walked Brendan and Pat. The three siblings all hugged each other and then immediately started arguing. Sister Kath tried to calm them all down, and Inspector Irvine was glad to usher them out of the office and onto Springfield Road as quickly as possible. No one noticed Mary stuffing the slip of paper into her pocket as they left.

Chapter Twenty-Seven

An ordinary-looking blue Ford Cortina with Northern Ireland plates drove slowly through the centre of Feeny, a tiny village in County Londonderry. A young couple were in the car, and a man at the wheel was smiling as he spoke to his companion in the passenger seat. Mrs Regan watched the car drive past as she waited for her bus to take her to Dunliven for her monthly shop. She smiled to herself as she saw the man and the girl laughing together.

At least someone's happy! she thought. A lorry pulled out into the road and the blue Cortina stopped to give the lorry room to manoeuvre. *That's a handsome young man!* thought Mrs Regan. She looked at the girl who was smiling and relaxed in the passenger seat, also attractive, and maybe a few years older than her driver. Mrs Regan wondered briefly who they were. Perhaps they were married or perhaps they were having an affair?

The lorry had moved on, and the blue Cortina resumed its unhurried journey, although the young couple seemed much more interested in each other than reaching their destination.

Inside the blue Cortina, there was real tension in the air. Jenny might be smiling, but this was only to disguise the very serious instructions she was giving on the hidden radio to three other cars less than four miles away, which were also manned by operators. Colin was at the wheel beside her and had slowed down when they entered Feeny, so they were not too close to the target vehicle, which was just in front of them. Colin had to grind to a halt when the lorry unexpectedly drew out in front of them and both of them thought this might be an ambush.

"We're going to lose the target!" Jenny had a fake smile on her face, but her voice was very anxious.

"No, we won't," Colin replied quietly while grinning at the same time. *I might learn to be a ventriloquist when this is all over,* he thought. At the same time, he put the car into gear and moved off. As soon as he was clear of the village, he put his foot down on the accelerator and they could soon see the back of the red Hillman Hunter that was the target vehicle.

Jenny decided that a change of cars was needed, although she was sure that the target had not realised that it was being followed.

"Oscar Three, this is Oscar One; send location over," Jenny said. Oscar Three was another car under Jenny's control. Although they had left Feeny and no civilians were visible, both Colin and Jenny maintained happy facial expressions despite the strain they were both under.

"Oscar Three, two hundred metres south of Red Apple over." Over the past week, on a large map of the area surrounding the villages of Claudy, Feeny and Park, every crossroads and T junction had been given a code word that had to be memorised by Jenny's team – of which Colin was the second in command. Red Apple was a T junction on the Feeny to Claudy road.

"Oscar One, roger. Tango will be at Red Apple in figures four; take it on over."

"Oscar Three Wilco out."

"Oscar Two, this is Oscar One. Send location. Over."

"Oscar Two, Blue Apple over."

"Oscar One, roger out."

This exchange of messages meant that Oscar Three – a battered red Cortina driven by Barry – should start following the target when it passed the T-junction on the Feeny to Claudy road. Oscar Two was another car already in Claudy where the target was headed. Jenny's team had learned the hard way that it was equally important to have a car in front of the target as well as behind it.

Both Jenny and Colin were armed to the teeth. Both had a .22 calibre Walther PPK in a small holster around their right ankle. Colin's main weapon was an army-standard 9mm Browning in a shoulder holster underneath the left side of his denim jacket. Jenny had a machine pistol under the right side of her leather jacket. Colin was still unsure of its manufacturer and suspected it might be a hybrid, but he had seen Jenny use it on the range and it was a ferocious weapon. Colin also had two unexpected pieces of weaponry. The military police did not like operators to carry their personal penknives or commando daggers, so one evening after patrol, under the pretext of looking for some eggs in the cookhouse to make an egg banjo, Colin had 'borrowed' a small kitchen knife from the cookhouse, which he had since sharpened and strapped under the right sleeve of his denim jacket in a makeshift holder made largely from black masking tape. He had also signed for an extra Walther from the armoury and this was hidden in his left sleeve, again, strapped with masking tape to prevent it from slipping down his arm. All their weapons were made ready, or cocked, with only the safety catch preventing a negligent firing. Colin remembered being ticked off for having weapons made ready before the shooting in Colinward Street, and here they were now, with cocked weapons being the norm.

"Where will the target go when it reaches Claudy?" Jenny asked. "On to Derry?"

"Intelligence thinks it might be Strabane," Colin replied.

"Slime, don't get it all right but better be safe," said Jenny, then on the radio. "Oscar Four, this is Oscar One. Move to Grey Apple. Over."

"Oscar Four Wilco out."

Oscar Four was a car with just one operator inside, and Grey Apple was a crossroads just south of Claudy.

Colin was rather pleased that Jenny had taken his advice that Strabane was a possible target destination. Anything he had said when they first went to Northern Ireland was rejected out of hand. But now they were getting along better. He risked a glance to his left and was relieved to see that she looked calmer than when they had had to stop in Feeny.

Both of them were wearing clothes bought second-hand from shops in Northern Ireland. Colin was wearing a grey denim jacket and blue jeans, both of which needed a wash. His hair was dirty and shoulder-length, and he hadn't shaved for three days. Jenny looked smarter; her leather jacket might be second-hand, but it was well made. She wore a blue T-shirt under her jacket that fitted her a little too tightly, showing off her breasts unnecessarily. Colin thought she looked too good; after all, she was on surveillance duties in rural Co Londonderry, not auditioning for a Bond movie.

"Oscar One, this is Oscar Four; tango heading south towards pink apple. Over!"

The message crackled in Colin's hidden earpiece urgently.

Jenny responded immediately, "Oscar One, roger, take on tango. Over."

"Oscar Four Wilco out."

So it was going to be Strabane! Jenny spent the next few minutes reorganising her team so that there was a car both in front and behind the target heading south. Jenny and Colin also turned south towards Strabane. In no time, the unremarkable blue Cortina had reached Dunnamanagh, and they should be in Strabane in less than thirty minutes. Colin had never been to Strabane but was of course intrigued because it was Mary's home town, not that he was going to mention this to Jenny, who was sitting beside him anxiously.

They were both quiet in the car, deep in thought and concentration. Then Jenny spoke, "Intelligence said the target is running weapons or explosives, but we don't know who to blame yet. I want us to get to Strabane before anyone else to make a plan. As quick as you can, Colin!"

Colin didn't need a second invitation. He shoved his foot down on the accelerator and they hurtled south along narrow roads towards Strabane. The big question now for Jenny, as team leader, was what the destination for the target was. There were two main possibilities; the Ballycolman Estate or the Townsend, both of which were strong Republican areas where the target could get assistance. A big factor was the Mourne River that flowed through the centre of the town, with the Ballycolman Estate to the west of the river and the Townsend to the east. The Ballycolman was by far the largest of the two estates and would offer better protection for the target than the Townsend, but the target would have to cross the Army Checkpoint Bravo on Bridge Street to reach the Ballycolman. This may not be a problem if the target vehicle was not yet carrying weapons or explosives, but it would be if the plan was to take delivery in the Ballycolman and then transport their cargo to the east of the river to Londonderry or even Belfast.

Jenny quickly made her plan, which she discussed with Colin as he drove at breakneck speed southwards. "I'm going to put two cars west of the Mourne River in case it's the Ballycolman. Then Barry goes up north in case they're headed to Derry, while we stay around the town centre to cover the Townsend."

"OK," Colin replied. "I'd better inform the ops room of what we're doing so they can brief the SF on the ground."

"Do it now," said Jenny abruptly. Colin had made a good point and Jenny knew this. Strabane was a dangerous town for the Army and the RUC, and it had witnessed a litany of IRA killings in the past. As a result, the security forces maintained a force of company strength based at the RUC station in the centre of town, with an extra platoon based in Sion Mills to the west of the Mourne River. The Army patrolled the streets frequently, and there was the danger that one of these could intercept one of Jenny's cars in the belief that they might be IRA. Orders would probably be given to the troops on the ground to cease patrol activity and to restrict activity to manning the static checkpoints on the Mourne River and the border crossing to Lifford in Donegal.

With Colin at the wheel, they made it to Strabane with time to spare before the target arrived, and they decided to park up near the centre of town and wait. Less than ten minutes later, the Hillman Hunter was reported in Barrack Street, and Jenny radioed her team to tell them that her car would take over – following the target from behind. Colin had to be very careful not to be too close to the target, who they had been following in Feeny earlier that day. Then the target turned south! So it was going to be the Townsend!

"All stations Oscar, this is Oscar One, target in Fountain Street, Townsend Estate. Wait Out!" Jenny's voice was controlled but Colin could sense the nervous tension that she was struggling to control.

"Colin, keep on the target," Jenny ordered. Colin could see the target clearly up the road, which was moving slowly along Fountain Street. The Townsend Estate was long and narrow and at the foot of a steep valley. Hills on either side looked down on the estate and Colin felt vulnerable. The target vehicle stopped outside one of the terraced houses in the street, and Jenny ordered Colin to continue and pass the vehicle without stopping. As they drove along the street, they saw two people leave the car and walk quickly inside a terraced house, which could be either 45 or 47 Fountain Street. Jenny managed to take a photograph with a hidden camera, which might help when they returned to base. Jenny's team could now not linger anywhere in the Townsend Estate; it was too small, and a strange car would be noticed if they made another pass along Fountain Street. They had followed the target halfway across the province to Strabane. It was time to return to base.

Chapter Twenty-Eight

"So why the panic, Iain?" asked Ciaran. Munro's decision to use two red drawing pins and activate the emergency procedure was risky for both of them, and Ciaran was nervous. They were both sitting in the Waterside Hotel's lounge on Limavady Road, in eastern Londonderry. This was a quiet neutral spot that was relatively safe for both of them, and there was an unwritten agreement between the security forces and Sein Fein that the hotel could be used for low-level meetings to keep lines of communication open. But Ciaran still felt vulnerable and wanted to keep the meeting short.

"The vetting people have contacted me and want to interview me tomorrow. They're going to ask me all about my parents."

"Your parents are now both dead, Iain," Ciaran replied. "As you told the Army when you first joined."

"But these people are doing positive vetting; they will want much more detail. They will contact my cousin as well, who knows about my childhood in Northern Ireland."

"Oh come on Iain. He knows nothing about your real childhood, only the trips to Scotland. He knows nothing about your visits to see me when he thought you were staying with school friends."

But Munro was still worried. "He still knows my mother was born in Strabane, in a Republican area."

"Yes, but after your mother died, when you were just nine, he didn't know about your trips to Ireland. We kept your visits very quiet. Since university, you haven't even set foot in Northern Ireland until your current posting. All our meetings were held in rural Wales or bloody Scotland."

"I still don't like it."

"Look, what's the worst that can happen? If you fail the bloody vetting, what will the Brits do? Send you to another posting, maybe where you won't see anything so secret. But you'll still be helpful to us."

Munro didn't answer and looked unhappy.

After a moment, Ciaran added. "There's something else troubling you, isn't there?"

Munro stared into his pint of lager.

"Bloody Colin Smith is in Northern Ireland. Worse still, he's in Derry."

"How do you know?"

"I saw him with my own eyes." Right in the middle of Ebrington barracks, and by the Pay Office for fucks sake."

"He's always been trouble. Perhaps we can do something about it. But what's so important about the Pay Office?"

"Nothing." Munro sighed. "But there's an office above, always locked."

Ciaran thought rapidly, *It would be good to kill the English bastard Colin Smith, who always turned up at the wrong time.* He could see that Munro was losing his cool and he wanted to finish the meeting quickly. But first, he needed more information.

"What's so important about the Pay Office?" Ciaran persisted.

"I told you. Nothing. But, there's a secret room above it that's always locked."

"OK, what happens in this secret room?" Ciaran was also now beginning to lose his cool.

"It's where the undercover people go sometimes."

"To do what?"

"I don't know, but the general goes there to meet them."

"You haven't told me about this before."

"I haven't had the chance, have I?" Munro replied tetchily.

"Look," Munro continued. "The undercover people have to report to the general on a regular basis. They don't like meeting at the headquarters because they don't want to be seen, even by their own side. So, they have this secret room where they can usually meet in the evening when the pay office is closed, and that bit of the barracks is deserted."

"Have you been inside this special room?" asked Ciaran.

"Not a chance. Only the general goes, usually with his chief of staff. But last time, another man who I've never seen before joined them because of what's happening in Strabane."

"Strabane? What's happening in Strabane?"

"I keep telling you, Ciaran. I'm not included in meetings about special forces. I just try to eavesdrop without raising suspicion. All I've overheard are Feeny, Claudy and Strabane. Oh, and the Townsend, that's an estate in Strabane, isn't it?"

"Yes, Ian," said Ciaran thoughtfully. "In our home town."

Chapter Twenty-Nine

Colin drove out of Ebrington Barracks onto the Limavady Road and headed south towards Strabane. Colin realised that he had not enjoyed his initial meeting with General Sir Jocelyn. His previous briefing session had been with the Brigadier commanding 7 Brigade, who was easy to talk to despite his seniority and he was also a good listener. General Sir Jocelyn had neither of these two strengths; instead, he liked to talk down to his juniors, displaying a massive ego. He was also a bad listener, constantly interrupting with his views without taking stock of what he was being told. As a result, sitting in the cramped room above the Pay Office in Ebrington Barracks, Colin struggled to explain how fragile the surveillance situation was in the Townsend, an estate that was so small that any unusual cars or watchers on foot could easily be spotted. The meeting was all the more awkward because the general was another Guards officer and had served in Colin's regiment before being promoted to the staff. As such, there should have been a natural bond between the two officers, but this was absent during their meeting. To make matters worse, the general had sprung on Colin the news that Munro was now his ADC and that perhaps it would be fun if the three Guards officers could have supper together one evening; if he was not too busy. Colin could think of nothing worse. He had not taken a fancy to General Sir Jocelyn, and he did not like Munro. He remembered Johnny Keynsham telling him that the general had not been very popular in the regiment despite his undoubted ability. He was not sure how much Munro was liked either, despite his largesse with house parties to Scotland, from which Colin was always excluded. Feeling rather guilty, Colin wondered if the regiment had on purpose placed two of their least popular officers together as far away from Chelsea Barracks as was possible.

Anyway, he was too busy for supper parties. Keeping watch over the target car and the house in the Townsend was proving difficult and was stretching the team's resources to the full. They had left their main base near Ballykelly and had set up a temporary camp in some farm buildings just north of Strabane. This made them vulnerable, and Jenny knew that they could not camp there too long without being discovered. They had prepared a cover story about filming a documentary for television to buy them a little more time. They had thought of basing themselves at the RUC station in the centre of Strabane, where an infantry company was also located, and this would have removed the need to guard themselves. But their cars would soon be spotted, and their cover blown.

"Oscar Bravo, this is Oscar Alpha. Send location. Over."

His hidden radio spoke to him urgently in his right ear. Colin glanced to his right and saw the River Foyle only yards away. "Oscar Bravo, Red Orange. Over," Colin replied. "Oscar Alpha, roger out." This brief exchange of radio messages meant that Jenny wanted to know that he had finished his meeting in Ebrington Barracks and was on his way back to Strabane. The team had memorised new code words for places, and "Red Orange" told Jenny that Colin was at a T junction on the Derry to Strabane road. But, most of all, Colin could tell from the tension in Jenny's voice that something was up.

He didn't have long to wait. "Oscar Bravo, this Oscar Alpha, blue Ford, registration starts Alpha India Bravo, heading north towards Derry, should be with you in figures 5; your target over."

Colin quickly acknowledged these instructions, but this could be difficult! The car he was driving was one that the team used to go to meetings in army bases, and it had to be assumed that it might be compromised by a terrorist watching the entrance to Ebrington Barracks. It was dangerous to use the same car to follow a target. Normally, cars used to follow targets had been nowhere near an army base. Then there was the fact that Colin had no idea who was in the car or where it had come from. He wished he had spent the day with the team in Strabane rather than wasting his breath on a senior officer.

Grumbling to himself, Colin found a lay-by with a good view of the road coming from the south and settled down to wait. He felt the familiar increase in adrenalin as he contemplated what he had to do. It was turning dark as he waited, and he hoped the target would arrive soon so that he could spot the car as he was parked on the side of the road without lights. Minutes later, he saw the blue Ford, and he pulled out to follow the vehicle in the direction of Derry. He could just make out the letters of the number plate, Alpha India Bravo, but even with his side lights on, he couldn't read the full registration without getting dangerously close to the back of the target car. As Colin drove, he gave regular reports on his radio, giving his location and what little he could see in the target car – one driver, size and shape unknown – and no passengers so far as he could tell. In about ten minutes, they were on the southwestern edge of Derry. The Rover Foyle was to Colin's left, but it was dark now, and Colin could see very little other than the blue Ford to his front. The car indicated right and turned up a steep hill into the outskirts of Derry; this was unfamiliar territory for Colin, who followed at a safe distance behind. Colin tried to send his location on his radio but could not get a signal. The car continued up the hill on a narrow and twisty road until, after about five minutes, it emerged onto a housing estate and turned right. As Colin followed, he drove past a large wall on which 'Brits Out' had been painted in white letters. "This must be the Gobnascale," said Colin to himself.

The Gobnascale was a slightly unusual housing estate, in that it was the only Republican estate on the east side of the Foyle. Perched on a hill, looking down on the Waterside area, it resembled a Roman Catholic enclave within the east of Londonderry that was otherwise fiercely Protestant and Unionist. As such, it was not the sort of IRA stronghold to be found on the west of the Foyle, such as the Creggan and Bogside, but it was still a dangerous place for an operator alone and out of radio contact. A minute later, the car turned into another road, which Colin could make out to be Anderson Crescent from a street sign next to an Irish tricolour that had been daubed on the side of a house. The car then stopped, and shortly afterwards a lone figure emerged and went into a house, but Colin could not see the house number in the gloom, if indeed there was a number. In frustration, Colin tried his radio again, but it was still not working. Colin knew he had to make a decision quickly. Without a working radio and by himself, he could not linger for long in a Republican estate. No one back in the ops room knew where he was. Colin decided to drive out of the Gobnascale until he found somewhere from where he could communicate, if necessary by telephone, if he couldn't get a radio signal. But first, he needed more information about the target. His orders had been to follow the car, and he should at least establish exactly where the occupant had ended up. He made up his mind to park his car and walk the short distance to where the target car was parked. At the very least, he wanted to see the number of the house into which the figure had entered and, ideally, a better description of both the house and the car. Colin would allow himself just one pass by the car and house. After double-checking the Browning under his shoulder and the smaller pistol strapped to his right ankle, he left his car, locked it, and walked at a steady pace directly towards the target car. He told himself, "You are responding to an ad offering a job. You've got an interview with Mr Malone. The ad said he was in number 47 Anderson Crescent." Colin tried to make himself believe his flimsy cover story. When he was just ten metres away from the car, a girl emerged from the house and walked rapidly towards it.

"Damn!" Cursed Colin to himself. "We're going to arrive at the car together!" He thought of crossing to the other side of the road, but he was too close, and it would look suspicious. The girl had opened the car door, collected something from inside and turned to return to her house, closing the car behind her. As she turned, she looked directly into Colin's face.

"Colin!" said Mary.

"Mary! What the?" Exclaimed Colin.

They stood staring at each other beside Mary's car for what seemed to be at least a minute. Mary recovered first. "Well, come inside; it's good to see you." Colin was pleased to see that she was smiling.

Once inside, they hugged and kissed, and both started talking at the same time. Words poured out in a torrent. Mary explained that she had had to stay in Northern Ireland because her mother was ill. Normally, she was nursing at the RVH, but this week she was on a course at the Altnagelvin Hospital just outside Derry. Mary offered to show Colin around the house; yet another shared digs with other medical and nursing students, but no one else seemed to be at home. When they came to Mary's bedroom, Colin entered for an instant and then turned to walk back out onto the landing, but Mary stood in the doorway, barring Colin's exit. She smiled up at Colin's eyes as she closed the door behind her with her left ankle.

Later, as they lay upon Mary's narrow bed, they both had the chance to talk about recent events more calmly. The last time they had seen each other was at the small drinks party in St James' Palace just before the bomb attack, but she made no mention of her telephone warning, which had probably saved his life. When it was Colin's turn to tell his story, he was surprised at how calmly Mary reacted. She was very interested in the bomb attack and asked who the army believed made the warning. She asked why Colin had not contacted her since then, and Colin told her about being confined to barracks and then literally flown off to a course at an undisclosed location on the Welsh borders. Surprisingly, Mary was not shocked that Colin was working in Northern Ireland, and she told him about her strange encounter with the man in RUC Springfield Road who had given her a telephone number to call if need be. Mary appeared to accept the role he had in Northern Ireland, but Colin dreaded the next question.

"But, Colin, what are you doing in the Gobnascale?"

"Well…" Colin stammered.

At that moment, there was a loud knock on the front door, and they both scrambled off the bed. Mary threw on some clothes and went downstairs.

"All right, I'm coming!" she shouted.

Colin also put on his clothes rapidly. Furthermore, he had to worry about his armoury that he had removed earlier. He quickly strapped the small pistol to his right ankle and fitted the 9mm into his shoulder holster. He thrust his knife and his spare .22mm pistol, which he normally carried in his sleeves, into one of his denim jacket's pockets. Making sure that he could draw his pistol rapidly, he carefully looked down the staircase to see who was at the door. He was instantly relieved to see that Mary knew the visitor, but he could tell that she brought serious news.

"Hello, Chloe. What brings you here?" asked Mary anxiously.

"It's your Ma, Mary. She's taken a turn for the worse; she's on her way up to the Altnagelvin now!"

Colin peered down the staircase. The girl, whom Mary had referred to as Chloe, had her back to Colin and was wearing a nurse's uniform. But she looked vaguely familiar.

"I've got my car outside. I can take you there now," Chloe offered. "We should get to the hospital just before your mother arrives."

"I'll get my coat; give me a sec." Mary was sounding flustered and turning to look up the stairs, she said loudly. "Colin, I've got to go to the hospital; my mother is in a bad way."

"Can I help at all, Mary?" Colin replied. As he did so, he looked down the stairs and caught Chloe's eye. She looked back at Colin, who was standing at the top of the stairs. It was not a friendly look.

"No, it's OK but I must be going." Mary replied.

"OK, Mary, hang on; I'll be going too," said Colin.

"I'll wait in the car," said Chloe with one more look at Colin before leaving through the front door to her car, which was just outside the house.

When Chloe had left the house, Colin turned to Mary, kissed her and said, "Promise me you'll tell me how you get on." Mary nodded. Then Colin reached inside his jacket for a small piece of paper, which he handed to Mary. "You can reach me on this number," he said.

"Why is it that all you Brits are giving me their telephone numbers?" Mary replied and walked across to the car outside.

Chapter Thirty

Ciaran left his crash meeting with Ian Munro both worried and excited. He was worried because Munro was clearly on edge and, as such, likely to make a disastrous mistake. At the same time, Munro's information about British special forces operating in Strabane was gold dust. The information was all the more valuable because it was so precise: the Townsend Estate, which of course he knew well, and so small! At the same time, it was very alarming that the Brits knew about the volunteers who were working in the area and had sent special forces to spy on them. He wished he could get Munro to find out more, but he couldn't press him any more than he had tried earlier. Munro was on edge enough as it was.

Ciaran had to decide quickly what to do with this new information. He was going to need Chloe to warn the volunteers in Strabane. He had told Chloe to keep a low profile after her work in London, and she had gone back to nursing, but she was available to act on his orders at short notice. He was also going to have to talk to Jerry, who, together with Ciaran, was the only other person who knew the real purpose of the operation in Strabane. The volunteers on the ground knew they had to move explosives from Strabane to Derry when ordered to do so.

But only Jerry and Ciaran knew that the explosives were earmarked for a bomb attack at Coleraine University, just thirty miles to the east of Derry. The Queen was due to visit the university in August 1977 and Munro had obtained details of the visit, which he had passed to Ciaran in secret.

Colin expected to be debriefed about the car he had been told to follow into Derry, and he had spent the drive back to Strabane rehearsing what he was going to say. Colin decided he was not going to lie but empathise the bits he had done correctly. Here, he did have some ammunition. He had followed the car, as ordered, into the Gobnascale Estate. He had made a note of the address and could, of course, describe the girl who had entered the property and who – about an hour later – was driven in another car to the Altnagelvin hospital. He had made a note of Chloe's car, which he followed to the hospital. It was true that he had lost radio signal in the Gobnascale, despite its location on top of a hill. He had managed to re-establish radio contact outside the Altnagelvin when he gave a summary of what he had seen before being told to return to their base in Strabane as soon as possible. As it happened, and much to Colin's initial surprise, he was not closely questioned upon his return. The team's intelligence officer noted that, as ordered, Colin had followed a car to an address in the Gobnascale. The driver had stayed in the house for just over an hour before another car arrived, driven by a girl in a nurse's uniform. Then both girls drove to the Altnagevin hospital, at which point Colin was ordered to return to base. The intelligence officer did not give Colin much information about the car he was ordered to follow into Derry; other than that, it had been spotted leaving an address in Ballycolman Estate, known to be the home of Brendan and Pat Flynn, both IRA suspects.

Colin would have been subject to much closer questioning if it were not for the level of activity in the team's base. The pressure of maintaining covert surveillance on the house in the Townsend Estate was growing by the day, and tempers were becoming shorter.

The main concern was that the team was too stretched, with the same cars driving past the house in the Townsend at irregular intervals. They had requested additional cars and help from another team based near Belfast, but these requests had been denied by the DSF repeatedly with little explanation. Apart from occasional drive-pasts, there was little else the team could do to monitor the house, although the target vehicle was still parked outside the house. It was considered too risky to walk past the house in plain clothes because the presence of strange faces would probably be noticed by IRA dickers in such a small estate. Colin volunteered to join one of the regular army patrols that frequently patrolled the Townsend Estate anyway. This gave Colin the chance to walk straight past the house and the car to see if anything was of interest. This had to be approved by the DSF, who grudgingly agreed, and the infantry company based in Strabane was instructed to assist. Colin felt strange putting on his uniform again, and he had to smarten himself up by shaving and even trimming his hair so he could wear an army beret without looking ridiculous. But the downstairs blinds were drawn when Colin went by, and he could add nothing to what the team knew already. After a couple of weeks, it was becoming clear that some hard decisions had to be made. Their temporary base in the farm just north of Strabane was no longer secure, and a farmer from a neighbouring property had turned up recently, asking questions. The TV crew cover story was wearing thin. It had to be acknowledged that very little new intelligence had been gained since the car had arrived in Strabane. The only movement from the house had been an occasional return trip in the car to the Ballycolman, but this appeared to be more about collecting extra food and a change of clothing than transferring munitions. The car had been stopped at the Bravo checkpoint on one occasion, and a quick search revealed nothing sinister.

Major Smith made a rare visit to the team's camp and listened very carefully to what he was told. Colin had the impression that Major Smith, as he called himself, knew most of what he was told already. It was also obvious that he knew much more than the team about the suspects they were following. After about an hour of listening to the team, he drew Jenny to one side, and the two spoke to each other for another fifteen minutes out of earshot. Major Smith was then seen to leave without saying goodbye, and Jenny brought the team together.

"OK, we've made a decision," Jenny started. "It's now acknowledged that we can't keep going as we are without reinforcements, which we are not going to get. So, in twenty-four hours, we move back to our base at Greysteel. That means we make one more sweep of the target at 10.15 hours tomorrow." Colin could see the look of relief on Jenny's tired face, and the announcement was welcome news; one operator even cheered from the back of the room.

The next morning was bright and sunny and the warm weather, together with the knowledge that they would all soon be leaving Strabane, lifted everyone's spirits. There was a light-hearted end-of-term atmosphere at the morning meeting when Jenny gave her orders.

"OK, so it's very simple. Barry and I will be in Blue Tango One, and we'll enter the Townsend Estate from the west, just as before. We will drive past the target house with Barry at the wheel, and I'll try to take a concealed photo to see if anything is new."

"Colin, you will be Blue Tango Two and enter the Townsend Estate three minutes before we do and take a left up into Innismore Drive. From there, you'll be to our south and on higher ground, where you can get a good view of the estate."

Colin nodded in agreement. The team had done this many times in the last two weeks. Perhaps too many times.

"We'll have two more cars," Jenny continued. "Blue Tango Three is in the centre of town, and Blue Tango Four is to the east of the Townsend as a backup. Make sure you are all in position before 10.15 hours when Barry and I enter the estate."

There were no questions, and everyone got ready for the op. Three operators were not going on the task, and they would be in radio contact throughout. They were in particularly good spirits, and one of them had started loading up the team's equipment into their van, ready for the drive back to Greysteel.

Colin checked his equipment; the radio fitted in the car, another radio in his clothing with a hidden earpiece and his armoury. The standard-issue 9mm Browning pistol was his main weapon. It was so familiar after the weeks spent on the ranges, and he knew that what he aimed at he would hit.

When Colin left the makeshift camp, he noticed, not for the first time, how pretty the countryside in County Tyrone looked as soon as the sun shone. He caught a glimpse of the Mourne River sparkling in the morning light, and he found it hard to reconcile the picture around him with the lethal tools of his trade that he had hidden about his body. He was on time, so he decided to enter the Townsend Estate from the east via Milltown Road. The roads were quiet, with only an occasional tractor or lorry as he drove the last two miles before entering the estate. He passed a farmyard on his right, with a tractor sitting at its entrance with the engine running. When Colin drove past, the tractor pulled out and trundled down the road behind Colin's car. As soon as he was in the estate, Colin turned left up the hill into Springfield Street, where he stopped. He could see most of the estate from where he was parked. He decided to risk stepping away from the car for a moment to gain a better view by climbing a small bank on the side of the road. From his vantage point, Colin could see where he entered the estate; the tractor had stopped and was now blocking the road. There was no sign of the driver. Colin then looked to the left and very shortly saw Jenny's car enter the Townsend from the west before driving slowly towards the target house on Townsend Street. Colin looked closely at the car; he could easily see Barry at the wheel and could just make out the shape of Jenny sitting to his left and moving in her seat. *Perhaps she is adjusting her hidden camera,* thought Colin, before looking back to his left from where Jenny's car had entered the estate. Suddenly, in a matter of seconds, the situation changed for the worse. A large lorry with a pile of rubble on its rear had parked at the entrance to the estate and was offloading its cargo into the middle of the road, making it impossible for any vehicle to either enter or leave the estate from the west. Colin quickly glanced to the east. "Damn!" he said out loud. The wretched tractor was still blocking the east-facing road. They were trapped. Colin scrambled down the bank to his car, collected a pair of binos from the glove compartment, and ran back up the ramp to his vantage point. He could see that the tractor to the east had been abandoned and no one appeared to be in or close to the vehicle. The large lorry to the west was also deserted. He then trained his binos on Townsend Street and saw, for the first time, a white van stop one hundred metres in front of Jenny's car. Something long and black was lying across the road.

"Calthrops! Damn it!" Colin cursed. "We're supposed to use them against the IRA, not the other way round." Caltrops, a long line of spikes attached to a piece of string, were so simple yet so effective. They could easily puncture all four tyres and Jenny's car was heading straight for them. Colin tried to radio a warning, but Jenny was not responding. He turned back towards his car, where there was a more powerful radio, only to see the windows shatter from gunfire. Colin looked to his right, and just ten metres away, he saw two balaclava-dressed gunmen armed with Armalites reloading their weapons. They had just emptied their magazines into Colin's car, apparently thinking he was still inside. Colin did not hesitate. Without shouting a warning, and before they could reload their weapons, he drew his Browning and fired two rounds at each gunman. They both dropped. It was very good shooting; even the instructors at the Close Quarter Battle Ranges in Wales would have been impressed.

Colin had to warn Jenny and the team that they were caught in a trap. He ran over to the two gunmen he had shot; they were either dead or dying and he grabbed their two Armalites which he was going to need. He then ran back to his car, which was covered in broken glass, jumped in and managed to start the car. He sent a contact report over the radio, but it was not acknowledged, and Colin could not be certain that it had been received.

Colin drove the car brutally down the hill; he was furious, and he had to get to Jenny's car immediately. He reached Townsend Street and was horrified to see that Jenny's car had hit the caltrops and was stationary at an awkward angle in the middle of the road. From the white van, three people emerged, all armed with what looked like Armalites and started to approach Jenny's car cautiously. There was no sign of movement from within the car and Colin guessed both Barry and Jenny must have hurt themselves when they hit the caltrops. One of the gunmen fired a burst of rounds into Jenny's car, shattering glass over the bonnet and the road. Colin fired two rounds from his Browning. The distance was too far to score a hit, but it did at least make the gunmen step back and take cover. Colin knew it would not take long for the gunmen to find a new firing position and open fire on Jenny's car again.

Colin had to get to the car to see if Jenny or Barry were still alive. There was a ditch on one side of the road, into which Colin jumped, offering some cover. He quickly checked the Armalites thankful that he had been made to fire them during training. After firing ten rounds rapidly to where he thought the terrorists were hiding, he sprinted towards the car, surprised and thankful that he was not drawing their fire. However, when he reached the car, shots were only narrowly missing him. He opened Jenny's door and saw that she was bleeding badly from her shoulder, but she was still alive. Barry's head was a mess, as he had been hit several times in the head. He was very dead. Colin saw Jenny's machine pistol on her lap; she had perhaps tried to use it when the ambush was sprung. Colin grabbed the weapon and checked the magazine. Shots were now hitting the car more frequently, and Colin could see three gunmen moving steadily in his direction. One of them would take up a firing position and cover the other two as they edged forward. They had some infantry training.

It was time for Jenny's machine pistol. Colin waited a little longer until they were only a few yards away, and then fired a long burst at the approaching gunmen. Colin was amazed by the impact as the rounds spread over a wide area. He didn't think he had hit anyone, but the gunmen backed off in the face of the machine pistol. Jenny's pistol offered the only chance of escape. He could do nothing for Barry, but Jenny was still alive and bleeding heavily. Using the front passenger door as a flimsy cover, he dragged her out of the car, trying to ignore her screams of agony. He fired another long burst, raking the road to his front, put Jenny into a fireman's lift and ran as fast as he could back to his ditch. It was only a few yards to the ditch, and Jenny was not heavy, but it still seemed to take a lifetime to reach his cover. Once he thought he felt something thud into his back, and he wondered briefly if he had been hit.

Finally, he reached his ditch, and they slumped inside. Jenny didn't look good at all. One of the Armalites was where he left it, and he fired several rounds to keep the gunmen at bay. He also did his best to stem the bleeding from Jenny's shoulder. He still had her machine pistol, which he was going to need if the gunmen got closer. Shots were coming quickly in his direction, but the gunmen were too far for the machine pistol. He turned to the two Armalites; one of the magazines was jammed, but he was able to reload the other. He didn't know how long he could hold out in his ditch with Jenny bleeding to death at his side. Colin didn't know how long he spent in his ditch; later, he remembered using the Armalites at least once more to keep the enemy at bay, but he didn't have to use the machine pistol. Colin continued trying to stop the blood from Jenny's wound, and she was barely conscious. Colin passed out as well at one point, and when he woke, he heard voices, but these were English voices with northern accents. Suddenly, he looked up and found himself staring down the barrel of a rifle, but it was an SLR, not a bloody Armalite, and it was held by a sergeant in the fusiliers, his red plume bright in the morning sun. The sergeant looked down at Colin briefly before speaking into his radio. Colin heard him say, "We're going to need medics here, now!" and then something else before he passed out.

Chapter Thirty-One

There had been over a hundred mourners in the church, and even more followed her mother's coffin – draped in the Irish tricolour – on its way to the graveside. Mary would have been content to do without the tricolour, but Brendan and Pat had insisted that the widow of a volunteer who had died in the struggle against the Brits should receive this honour. At least she had been informed that there would be no masked IRA gunmen firing their pistols in the air at the graveyard. The Brits were keeping a watch from a distance, and Mary could hear the engine from one of their helicopters flying overhead. After the service, nearly everyone headed back to their house in the Ballycolman Estate to pay their respects, which involved some heavy drinking. The house was too small for everyone to fit inside, and some guests grabbed a drink and pushed their way through to the tiny garden. There was little money to spare for refreshments, but Brendan and Pat had managed to provide plenty of alcohol from somewhere. Mary had hoped that the death of their mother would bring her closer to her two brothers, but this had not worked out. She found that she could talk happily enough with Pat by himself, but he spent so much time with Brendan, who was such a dangerous influence. Nearly all of the mourners were from the estate, and only a handful had come from outside Strabane. Chloe was there, and it was the first time she'd seen her since she had driven her to the Altnagelvin hospital just before her mother died. There was another face she had not seen for a long time, Ciaran Maguire, who had known her father. She remembered him from her childhood, when the girls on the estate laughed at him behind his back because he looked like a rat. *He still looks like a rat,* Mary thought, *Just an older one.* Ciaran, Brendan and Chloe spent a lot of time in a corner whispering to each other, but she had no idea about what.

The next morning, Mary woke up early. She had not drunk very much after the funeral, and her head was surprisingly clear. There was no sign of Brendan or Pat, and Mary guessed that her two brothers had dossed down with some IRA cronies to sleep off their sore heads while leaving their sister to sort out their mother's belongings. In truth, there was little for Mary to do. What few possessions her mother had owned were worth very little but would have to be boxed up and removed in the next few weeks. Mary decided to start upstairs and work downwards. Her mother's bedroom smelt damp, and the bed linen needed to be washed thoroughly if it was going to be retained. Her mother's clothes were also damp, and her possessions were pitifully few. Beside the bed, there was a framed photo of her mother and father taken on their honeymoon in Co Donegal. Both of them looked well and smiled happily for the camera, blissfully unaware of the life of hardship that awaited them. Mary looked through the bedside drawers and the cupboard before heading downstairs. So far, apart from the photo of her parents, there was very little she wanted to keep. She had decided to make a pile of things that should be retained on the table in the sitting room, and she added the photo to the meagre pile. In the bottom of a dresser in the sitting room, Mary found a large cardboard box that turned out to be full of photographs and a large album. She looked through the album, intending to skip through it quickly, but soon became engrossed. It pictured the very early days of her parents' marriage and the arrival of Brendan, Pat and herself. Mary recognised her mother's writing, and her early entries were neatly presented, which suggested some tender love and effort. Sadly, as the years passed, her mother's handwriting grew worse and was eventually unreadable. The photos had been neatly glued to the front of the album but were a mess towards the back. Nevertheless, Mary soon found herself looking through the photos, interested to see who had been around during her childhood. As well as Mary and her siblings, there were also snaps of her parents' friends.

Mary was interested to see that these included a few photographs of Ciaran, and in one snap, he was standing beside an attractive young girl who smiled at the camera. Mary guessed that they were brother and sister.

A knock at the door brought Mary back to the present day. She opened it, only to find that it was Chloe who said she was just calling in on her way back to work. This was kind, and Mary spoke to her for a few minutes before Chloe left for work and Mary went back to her clear out. She decided to put a stop to looking through the photos for now, but she wanted to keep them safe, together with the album, so that anyone in the family could look at them in the future. The little pile of her mother's belongings that Mary wanted to keep looked larger once the album and the box of photos were added. As Mary put the box on the table, a small photo that must have been stuck to the box's bottom fluttered to the floor. Mary leant down and added it to the others on the table, glancing at it briefly. Something had caught her eye. She picked it up and looked at the photo more closely. It was a snap of two people, one of whom was well-known, Ciaran Maguire. Ciaran had his arm on the shoulder of a boy, who looked to be about ten years old. Both Ciaran and the boy were looking directly at the camera, trying to smile. In Ciaran's case, he still looked like a rat, and in the boy's, there was something supercilious in his smile. Mary knew where she'd seen that look before, and she knew she had to do something about it.

The days that followed the violence in the Townsend Estate were the worst that Colin had ever experienced. Barry was dead, and Jenny was in a critical condition in Musgrave Park. The bodies of the two gunmen that Colin had shot and killed by his car were recovered and identified as suspected members of the IRA, but of those who had shot up Jenny's car, there was no sign. Everyone was shocked by the extent to which the IRA ambush had been planned. Vital and secret information had been passed to the IRA, which made the security forces look inept and vulnerable. It would now be impossible to find out what had been hidden in the Townsend Estate, as the occupants of the terraced house, which had been under surveillance, were long gone. Difficult though it was to admit it, one had to give credit to how well the ambush had been executed. To some extent, the security forces had played into the IRA's hands by operating undercover in such a small, narrow estate with steep hills on both sides. A supposedly broken-down lorry or tractor was all that was needed to stop any vehicle from entering or leaving the estate. The terrorists had also arranged for a large fuel truck to have a flat tyre right in front of the main entrance to RUC Strabane. Needless to say, the driver said he was not carrying a spare tyre. As soon as reports of gunfire had been received, the Army company had tried to move the vehicle, but this proved to be a nightmare when a group of youths appeared from nowhere, hurling half-bricks and petrol bombs towards the recovery vehicle. By the time it was cleared, army patrols on foot and running as fast as they could had already reached the Townsend Estate, in time to rescue Colin and Jenny but too late to save Barry or hurt the IRA.

Jenny's team had been stood down following the Townsend debacle. With their leader seriously wounded in hospital and one of the team members dead, they were not considered fit to mount operations. Then, there were all the questions that needed answering. And so it was that, yet again, Colin found himself under the scrutiny of the Royal Military Police. Their questioning was every bit as tough as it had been in the past, and, if anything, in the knowledge that one of their own was barely conscious in Musgrave Park, the questions were even more rigorous. Major Smith visited their base a few times, listening carefully to the various briefings without giving anything away himself.

Colin was made to have a full medical. However, despite some cuts from the glass that had shattered over his car, he was unharmed, at least physically. He asked several times for permission to visit Jenny in the hospital, but this was denied, and no reason was given. He volunteered to speak to Barry's family, but, again, this was denied. With Jenny's team standing down, Colin spent most of the time in the unit's ops room, where he kept watch and spoke at length about Northern Ireland with the Ops Officer Steve, who had also been an operator previously.

One morning, when Colin was the duty watchkeeper, one of the four telephones on the desk rang. It was called the Green Telephone, a secure line from either Brigade Headquarters, DSF, or even Headquarters Northern Ireland in Lisburn.

"Ops Room," Colin answered promptly.

"This is Iain Munro. The general wants to see you, Smith, as soon as possible."

"Hello, Iain, and how are you?" Colin replied calmly, despite the abrupt tone coming from Munro.

"When can you get here?" Munro continued, making no attempt to be civil.

"Doesn't the general want to be briefed by the new section head?"

"No!" Munro was becoming irritable. "He wants to see you. You were the one on the ground when the fiasco happened." The accusation that Colin was solely responsible for all that had gone wrong was clear. No mention of trying to save Jenny's life, of course.

"All right, Iain," Colin replied, suppressing a sigh. "When do I report?"

"Two p.m. this afternoon."

"At Ebrington, in the usual place?"

"No, the general wants to meet you at his residence in Clooney Park. More private. See you then."

Colin didn't like visiting Army barracks in Northern Ireland except for the secret camp where he and his fellow operators were based. The first concern was that an IRA watcher would note the details of his car when entering the base or, still worse, manage to take a photograph either of him or his car or both. One way around this problem was to be picked up by an army vehicle at some pre-arranged time and place and then travel to the barracks in the back of the vehicle, well out of sight. But this took a bit of time to plan, and time was usually something that Colin had little to spare. The second concern, and, to Colin's mind, the biggest danger, was being noted within the barracks itself. The big army barracks employed civilian staff to work in areas such as the Officers' Mess and Sergeants' Mess, and although everyone working on MOD property had been vetted, there was no guarantee that sensitive information would not be passed to the IRA. A friend of Colin's who had been stationed in Ebrington barracks realised one night on patrol in the Gobnascale Estate that the man he was searching for weapons also worked in the Officers' Mess.

As a result, Colin was both irritated and anxious when the general's ADC, Munro, phoned him earlier in the Ops Room to say that the general wanted a briefing in his Clooney Park residence outside Ebrington Barracks at two p.m. Munro was insistent, saying that the general wanted a debrief on the recent ambush when Number 47 was shot dead and Jenny was seriously injured. At least he was not driving into a barracks, but if the general's house was being watched, then his car would be compromised. For this reason, Colin was driving a pool car used for purposes such as visiting a barracks, not one of the vehicles used to patrol in very hostile areas. Clooney Park was a quiet cul de sac off the Limavady Road in a mainly Protestant district of Londonderry. The house was easy to spot as there were a couple of sangars on the perimeter, manned by soldiers from Ebrington Barracks. Colin drove up to the front gate and showed his ID card to a bored-looking private on duty, who looked at his face briefly to check that it matched the photo on the MOD Form 90. From inside the perimeter, Colin could see that the general's house was very large, with a wide driveway where two cars were already parked: a staff car and a Ford Cortina with Northern Ireland plates, which Munro must have used for the short trip from Ebrington Barracks. *The general's staff car must be inside the garage,* Colin thought as he climbed out of his car and went up a few steps to the front door. Colin rang the bell, and the door opened immediately, making Colin wonder if Munro had been waiting for him to arrive.

"The general is in the study. You are to go through immediately. Leave your weapons on the hall table. Including that thing you wear around your ankle." Munro ordered abruptly.

"I'm delighted to see you too," Colin replied with some sarcasm. "Can I go to the gents first?"

"First door on the left, past the telephone. Join us as soon as you can."

As Colin entered the gents, his radio crackled in his ear. He had forgotten to remove the earpiece from his ear when he had arrived, and it was designed to be unnoticeable to anyone other than other operators who knew what to look for.

The message was very direct. "Ring the Ops Room, immediately." He did not know what this was about, but he could tell it was important. As he left the gents, he saw the telephone that he had passed earlier. Colin looked around briefly for Munro to ask if he could use the telephone, but he must have been in with the general, so he picked up the receiver anyway and rang the number he had memorised long ago. After a couple of rings, he heard the voice of the duty officer.

"Steve speaking."

"Steve, this is Colin; I was told to ring."

"Colin, I've had a Mary Flynn on the telephone. How on earth did she get our number?"

"What does she want?" Colin's emotions were in turmoil; he was thrilled that Mary wanted to talk to him but anxious about the circumstances.

"She wants you to ring her immediately. She's in a phone box for the next two hours. If it's engaged, keep trying." Steve gave him the telephone number, which Colin committed to memory.

Colin hung up. There was still no sign of Munro. Colin tried to ring the call box, but there was no reply. He tried again, and this time Mary answered.

"Hello, who is this?"

"Mary, this is Colin. What's going on?"

"Listen, I've got to be quick. That rude man, when we had drinks at the palace, I can't remember his name."

"Iain, Iain Munro."

"OK, yes. Well, I think he's a Provo. "I'm at my mother's, and I found a book with his photo from when he was a boy in Strabane."

Colin felt a shiver down his spine. It was not just what he heard that made the hairs stand up on the back of his neck; it was also the quiet sound of a door opening behind where he was standing. Munro was behind him.

Colin decided to play for time.

"All right, Steve, I'll get on with that when I return to base." Colin tried to sound convincing. He was holding the telephone receiver in his right hand, and with his back to Munro, he moved his left hand to his right sleeve, where his small pistol and knife were hidden.

There was a small gasp from the telephone. "He's there with you, isn't he? Are you in trouble?"

"Yes, absolutely," Colin replied.

"So where is the general then?" Colin asked, trying to sound nonchalant. If he could warn the general about Munro, that might help them both.

"After you, Smith," said Munro, pointing to the door. He was using Colin's surname, which did not bode well.

Colin pushed the study door, and the general was there in front of him. But he was trussed up like a turkey, tied to a chair, and his mouth was gagged. His face looked very red.

"Bloody hell, Munro!" That's the general; release him at once!"

"Oh, shut up, Smith! The general is going nowhere. By the time I've finished with you, neither will you. Sit down on that chair and put your hands on your knees." Munro had drawn a 9mm pistol, which he was now pointing at Colin. There was less than five feet between the two of them, and Munro was unlikely to miss at such short range.

Colin decided to bluster – anything to gain some time.

"Munro! Have you gone mad? Put that pistol down now!"

"No, grammar school boy, I've got plans for you, and that means this pistol stays where it is."

"What plans? And drop all the grammar school stuff. You come from a housing estate in Strabane. You're a fraud. You're nothing special."

"Oh, I've been looking forward to a little chat with you, Smith. We've got a bit of time, and I can now talk to you about my past. You won't be telling anyone after all. My father was a very wealthy man, and so is my cousin in Scotland. I always spoke about Scotland and my family's estates to deflect attention from my mother, who came from a slum in Strabane. She didn't have a penny in her name until she married my father to avoid a scandal."

Munro seemed happy to talk, giving an account of his early years and school. The longer he spoke, the more time he had to loosen the knife in his sleeve. Colin wanted to encourage him. "OK, so your parents were unhappy, but when your father died, you became a rich man. "Where did spying for the bloody IRA come from?" Colin asked angrily.

"The nearest thing to a parent I had was my uncle, Ciaran Maguire."

"Who the hell is he?"

"You won't have heard of him," Munro said with a smirk. "He maintains a very low profile, and he's a very senior intelligence officer for the IRA." He recruited me when I was just a boy. You see, I hated my prep school in England. When my father died, my mother wanted me to go to a day school in Strabane. But Ciaran saw things differently. This was an opportunity to put a spy in the heart of the hated English state. During the holidays, I always told the other boys that I'd be in Scotland. And so I did, but secretly I went to Ireland as well to meet Ciaran."

The door opened from the side of the hall, and in walked a young girl dressed immaculately in the uniform of a captain in the Women's Royal Army Corps. Colin recognised her at once as the nurse who had come to Mary's house in the Gobnascale to give her the news about her mother. Munro must have provided the uniform for her.

"Come in, Chloe," said Munro, turning towards her and giving Colin the chance to loosen both the knife and the pistol in his sleeve. Both weapons were now ready. That was the good news. The bad news was that Colin now faced two enemies instead of one. Too late, Colin remembered that he had seen Chloe before in Belfast at the shoot-out in the RVH.

"Smith, allow me to introduce you to Chloe, a friend of …"

"We've met," Chloe interrupted Munro. "This is the English bastard that killed Saraid at the Royal."

Munro looked a little flustered.

"Oh, yes," Munro continued. "You were lucky that day, grammar school boy. And at St James'. Chloe helped me prepare the bomb."

"Another of your fuckups, Munro; that bomb of yours didn't kill anyone."

Munro reddened. Colin wanted to keep him talking and try to force him into making a mistake. Munro was still pointing his pistol at Colin at short range, but his aim and stance were not steady. "Your luck has now run out, Smith." Munro liked the sound of his voice. "Ciaran and his friends want to have a long chat with you about that bomb warning and how your undercover unit operates."

"And I'm going to pay Mary a visit, too," Chloe added, smiling nastily.

"This is what is going to happen," said Munro. "Chloe is a nurse here, and she's going to drug you."

Chloe was carrying a small bag, from which she produced a leather pouch that she unfolded on the table in the centre of the hall. "When you're unconscious, we're going to carry you through a side door into the garage and bundle you into the boot of the general's staff car before we drive straight out of the front gate. "Chloe will be driving in her uniform, of course, and I'll be the vehicle commander in the front, playing my part as the bossy ADC."

"You've always enjoyed being unpleasant. It comes naturally to you, probably because of your school days. Bullied a lot, were you?" Colin was pleased to see him redden again; he had to get him to make a mistake.

"You won't be so smug in a few hours' time when we have you over the border, trussed up like a chicken, talking to save your life."

"What're you going to do with the general?"

"Shoot him, of course, and with your pistol, so you get the blame."

"What's the point of that? You're going to kill me anyway."

"To get the Brits chasing their tails."

"You're half a Brit yourself, Munro, and a traitor. You passed on information about the Townsend to the IRA. You'll never get away with this. Just because my pistol will be the murder weapon won't stop you from facing a lot of very tough questions, especially if I've gone missing."

"Doesn't matter," Munro shrugged. "Ciaran and I think it's time I leave the Army and skip the UK. The vetting people are delving into my past and asking awkward questions. Then there's you, the bloody grammar school boy who's now worked it all out with the help of your tart Mary."

"Who I will enjoy visiting when we've dealt with you," added Chloe nastily.

Munro turned to Chloe again. "Aren't you ready yet?" he asked irritably.

"Just a moment," Chloe replied.

"A word of advice, Chloe; I don't think Munro likes girls," said Colin.

Munro was losing his composure. He had made Colin sit on a wooden chair, still with his hands on his knees. He had had to leave his main weapon and his ankle pistol on the hall table when he first arrived. That left him with only his knife and another small pistol in his sleeve. While

Chloe was assembling her syringe, Colin took a moment to review his predicament. He remembered the words of Wayne, the SAS sergeant and unarmed combat instructor, who had told Colin that if he ever found himself facing a gunman with a drawn weapon at close range he was "*in deep shit*." Munro was only a few feet away, which definitely counted as 'close range'. Colin also remembered grimly that Wayne had offered no credible solution to facing a drawn weapon at close range. At the time, Colin's solution had been ridiculous, childish even, but that was on the course. This was for real. Chloe had finished her preparations and held up a long syringe, at the bottom of which was a needle that looked even longer. Colin knew he had nothing to lose.

"Iain, your flies are undone!"

For less than a tenth of a second, Munro looked down, and his pistol wavered. Colin threw himself to the left from his chair, which fell over with a crash on the hall floor. At the same time, he drew his knife from his sleeve and hurled it at Munro. It was a hurried lob rather than a controlled throw; nevertheless, the knife hit Munro on his right hand, making him drop his pistol, which skidded along the hall floor towards the front door. Both Colin and Munro rushed over to the weapon, colliding with each other as they did so. They both hit the floor together and started fighting each other like two rats in a sack.

Meanwhile, Chloe was looking for her syringe, which she had dropped when Colin had dived from his chair. She then saw that it had rolled along the hall floor and ended up under a desk a few feet away from where Colin and Munro were fighting.

Colin quickly realised that Munro was stronger than he expected. Perhaps it was all that swimming and striding across grouse moors in all weathers. Munro was trying to get Colin into a stranglehold and was close to success. Chloe had managed to retrieve her syringe and rushed over to where Munro and Colin were fighting. She tried to jab Colin with the needle, but the two men were struggling so wildly that she couldn't aim a jab at Colin without prodding Munro by mistake.

"Get my pistol!" Munro gasped the order to Chloe. Munro had now managed a stranglehold around Colin's neck, but his order to Chloe had made Munro loosen the pressure a little, allowing Colin the chance to drag his hidden pistol from his sleeve. The pressure on Colin's neck was now intense, but, with a heave, he managed to grip the handle and pull it into the open. Colin couldn't tell if the safety catch was on or off, but he pressed the end of the barrel into Munro's body, or what he hoped was Munro's body. He didn't want to shoot himself! Munro's grip was stronger and stronger, and Colin's vision was fading. He was in danger of passing out. Colin knew he had to act, and, summoning all his energy, he squeezed the trigger on his pistol. There was a loud bang, and with his ears ringing, Colin was not sure initially if he had shot Munro or himself. But the pressure on his neck had eased, and he slowly started to move. He was badly out of breath and did not know what to expect. Then, as he inched forward, Munro's body slumped onto the hall floor. There was a large red stain on his shirt, and blood was pumping out of his stomach like a broken drainpipe. Colin started to stem the flow of blood from Munro's wound and looked around for something to use as a bandage. Then he remembered Chloe, who had grabbed Munro's pistol and was walking quickly over to where Colin was lying. Despite the violence and the struggle, Chloe looked composed and in control. She was at point-blank range as she pointed the pistol downwards towards Colin's face. "This is for Saraid, you English pig!"

Then there was another bang, but this time much louder, and the whole room seemed to shake. Irrationally, Colin wondered if there had been an earthquake. His head was spinning, and the hall was a little smokey. Colin saw that Chloe was stunned, and her pistol was no longer pointing at Colin's face. Chloe looked down at her stomach, unable to comprehend the neat red dot above her tummy button, then another red dot immediately above the first, until there was a vertical line of red dots stretching from her stomach to her face. As she crashed to the floor, Colin saw two figures wearing balaclavas who had appeared from nowhere. They were both carrying submachine guns. One of them walked over to where Colin was lying and took off his balaclava. It was Wayne who had taught unarmed combat on Colin's course. He looked down at Colin and said, "You OK, boss? I thought I told you not to let anyone point a gun at you at point blank range."

Chapter Thirty-Two

"It was our agent Munro who told us that the Brits were following our ASU into the Townsend Estate in Strabane," said Ciaran.

Jerry nodded but said nothing. They were both walking along the Antrim coast, and it was a beautiful sunny day. Ciaran wished he was wearing sunglasses, and he had to squint to look at Jerry, who was wearing a pair of very dark sunglasses above his ginger beard that was turning grey. The combination of the two made it even more difficult than usual to guess what Jerry was thinking. An English family, including two children, passed them on the footpath. It was very unusual to see holidaymakers from England in Northern Ireland, but along the Antrim coast, on a warm day, the troubles felt miles away.

Ciaran felt he had to press his case further. "Thanks to Munro, we were able to ambush the Brits, and our men got away with the explosives."

"We don't know how the Brits knew about our people in Strabane in the first place," Jerry replied.

"I know, Jerry, but at least the explosives are safe."

"Yes, but will they be ready for the Queen's visit to Coleraine? It's going to be tight."

Ciaran didn't answer, and both men continued their walk in silence. After a minute, Jerry asked. "That young Brit officer. Smith, isn't it?"

"Yes, Colin Smith. He killed Saraid in the Royal and was in London when the palace bomb exploded."

"The telephone warning alerted the Brits. We still don't know about that, do we? Was he also responsible for killing our two boys in the Townsend?"

"Yes, we think so."

Jerry stopped walking and turned to face Ciaran. "I want him dead."

They resumed their walk in silence. After another minute, Jerry stopped again and took a deep breath. With a sigh, he said. "Ciaran, I want to thank you for all you've done for the struggle over the years. Your agent, Munro, gave us some really useful information. Look, Jean and I are having a party over in Donegal next Tuesday. It's our wedding anniversary; it would be great if you could join us."

"Thanks, Jerry, of course. I look forward to it."

Chapter Thirty-Three

"How did you know I was in trouble?" Colin asked.

"That girlfriend of yours, Mary Flynn," came the reply from Major Smith. "She rang the Ops Room again after she spoke to you when you were with Munro. I gave her the number to ring if she ever wanted to when I met her at RUC Springfield Road. I'd just hauled in her two brothers, Brendan and Pat, for questioning."

Colin now remembered Mary's last rather cryptic remark as she left the house in the Gobnascale. Something about Brits wanting to give her telephone numbers. If Major Smith had given Mary the telephone number, was it just possible that Major Smith did not know about Colin seeing her in the Gobnascale and also giving her the number to ring?

"Where is Mary now?" Colin asked.

"We don't know. She handed in her notice at the RVH, said goodbye to her flatmate, and left Belfast, maybe even Northern Ireland."

"I met her flatmate, Sister Kath, when I was in the RVH. I bet she knows where Mary is. I could go and ask her."

"No, you bloody well won't," Major Smith said. You are not leaving here until you fly out of Aldergrove tomorrow morning."

'Here' was Headquarters Northern Ireland in Lisburn, where Colin had stayed in the Officers' Mess ever since Munro and Chloe had been shot in the general's house. It was all very comfortable, but he was very much confined to barracks.

"Can I at least telephone her?"

"You can try. She gave our guys a real flea in the ear when they spoke to her."

"Can I go and see Jenny if she is well enough?"

"I might allow that. It should be safe enough."

"How's the general doing?"

"Oh, he's OK. He was shaken up when we first set him free, but grateful, of course. Even wants to put you in for a medal!"

"And Munro? Chloe?"

"Both dead. We are going to say that Munro has gone missing. You realise, Colin, that the official line has to be that the incident in the general's house never happened."

"Won't the general have something to say?"

"Not bloody likely. He won't want to admit that his ADC was an IRA spy. Anyway, he will be leaving Northern Ireland. The story will be that he's had some sort of nervous breakdown. Not far from the truth, actually!" Major Smith chuckled unkindly. He then stopped speaking, stood up from behind his desk, and walked over to the window of the tiny room that passed for his office.

He stared out over Thiepval Barracks. He appeared to be coming to a decision. He turned to face Colin. "I suppose I've got to thank you. You unmasked an IRA spy in our midst who could have done still more harm to us in the future. We also have to thank your girlfriend, who is in danger, by the way. The IRA will have worked out the link between you, her and Munro. You, of course, are in grave danger. My sources tell me that you are to be killed. The order has come from Ciaran Maguire, someone we knew nothing about until Munro told you about him, thinking you wouldn't live to tell anyone. For your own safety, we've got to get you out of Northern Ireland right away, and you need to spend some time out of the UK."

Colin was allowed to visit Jenny before his flight back to London. She looked thin and frail, but he was relieved to hear that her life was no longer in danger. Colin found it difficult to talk to someone who had been his instructor and a tough team leader, often hard on Colin, but who now lay vulnerable on a hospital bed.

"How is the team?" Jenny asked. Colin was not sure if she knew that her team had been stood down since Strabane.

"I'm confined to HQNI until they fly me back to the UK tomorrow, so I'm out of touch."

"And then?" Jenny asked.

"Heaven knows. Germany probably. They want me to be out of the UK for a while. I'm allowed a week's leave in the UK, apparently, so I can go and stay with my mother, who hasn't seen me for ages."

"I'm sorry we stopped you from going on leave from the course," said Jenny, smiling wanly.

"What about you, Jenny? Back to special duties once you're fit again."

"I don't know either, but my tour is almost over anyway." So maybe it's time to return to the military police and start thinking about the staff college exams."

A severe-looking nurse walked into the ward, interrupting their conversation to say that it was nearly time for Jenny's medication. *In other words, get out of my ward,* Colin thought to himself. He knew he had to leave and started to stand up, but not before Jenny put her hand on his. Her eyes were watery. "Thank you, Colin, for, well, everything. Stay out of trouble."

Colin's week on leave went by in a flash. He spent most of the time with his mother in Reading. He had been told to say absolutely nothing about his recent activities in Northern Ireland, and, in any case, he did not want to upset her with the truth about Strabane and his confrontation with Munro. So they chatted about her friends and her home life in Reading. She kept herself very busy and had injected new life into her accounting practice, which was now thriving.

They also spoke a good deal about Germany, and his mother was excited to hear about his new posting to Fallingbostel, which was near Hamburg in the north of West Germany. Sadly, this was a long way from Bavaria, where Colin's grandmother still lived.

Colin was surprised when his mother told him that Jeremy Kershaw had been to see her. He had called her out of the blue to ask if he could visit her one afternoon. A few days later, they met for a cup of tea and a relaxed chat.

"He clearly likes you more than me," Colin had said it grumpily.

"I don't know, darling," his mother had replied. "I think he thinks a lot about you." He'll be glad to have you back. Do you know he's been promoted?"

Colin nodded. The day before, he had reported to Birdcage Walk to see the Regimental Adjutant, who had brought him up to date with what was going on in the battalion. Jeremy's career was going very well. After only a short stint as a lieutenant colonel, he was now commanding the battalion stationed in Wessex Barracks, Fallingbostel. Colin was a little puzzled that the Regimental Adjutant had asked no questions about his recent tour in Northern Ireland, but had told him to report to the battalion in West Germany at the end of the week once his short leave was over.

Colin was sorry not to see his sister Sarah, who was away on holiday. She had a new boyfriend, but she had not introduced him to her mother, who didn't even know his name or what he did with himself. However, it sounded as if Sarah's medical studies were going well, and that she would be a doctor in due course. Of course, Colin was also anxious to talk to Sarah about Mary. They had been very good friends at medical school, and Colin wondered if Sarah had heard anything. He had tried ringing the telephone in the student digs, but, as usual, it rang unanswered.

Colin realised that his best chance of tracking down Mary was through Sister Kath. But this was not easy. He didn't have a telephone number for her house in Crocus Street, and he wasn't sure if she even had a phone in the house. That meant he had to try to contact her via the RVH. This proved to be difficult; the Royal was not in the habit of facilitating personal calls between their staff and a member of the public. Colin's English accent may not have helped. However, Colin was persistent and left several messages for Sister Kath to ring him at his mother's house in Reading. On his last evening before setting off for Germany the following day, his patience was rewarded, and Sister Kath rang. Colin liked Kath, who had nursed Colin after the bomb attack in Ardoyne, and he knew she was fond of Mary. But in terms of knowing where Mary had gone, she was not able to help.

Sister Kath had never told a lie in her life, and she was not going to start now. She liked the young Brit, Colin, and was glad to be truthful when answering his questions. When she told Colin that she had no idea where Mary had gone, she was telling the truth. When she said that one day after work she found a short note from Mary thanking her for everything and that she needed to go away, she was telling the truth. When she said that Mary needed to escape Northern Ireland, she was telling the truth. After all, Mary was caught in the middle between her two brothers, both IRA gunmen, and the sinister British intelligence officer,

Major Smith. Then there was her ambition to be a doctor, and she no longer needed to stay in Strabane to look after her mother. All this made sense, and Colin seemed to accept what Kath told him eventually.

But Kath was glad Colin didn't ask if she thought there were any other reasons why Mary had to depart suddenly. Kath was glad she didn't have to mention the envelope in Mary's pigeonhole at the RVH. Kath could tell which department had sent the letter just by looking at it. In fact, she knew what was going on anyway. Sister Kath hadn't spent her working life in the RVH, including a spell in midwifery, without knowing when a healthy young girl like Mary Flynn was in the early stages of pregnancy.

Chapter Thirty-Four

The three of them were in high spirits as they headed off to the border with Co Donegal. Brendan and Pat had arrived at Ciaran's flat just after eleven a.m., and the back seat of the car was stashed with bottles and cans of beer for the party. Pat was driving and stayed sober, but Brendan and Ciaran had started drinking as soon as they set off. As their spirits lifted, they even burst into a song, one of their favourites, which was about English soldiers coming in the middle of the night to take away their children.

They were still noisy as they approached the British army checkpoint known as the Hump, which stood on the border with Strabane and Co Donegal. Their car was clean, and nobody was carrying weapons or explosives, but they still expected to be stopped and searched by the Brits as the Flynn brothers were IRA suspects. As it happened, though, the Brits just checked Pat's driving licence while a bored-looking sentry took a brief look inside the boot of the car, only to find more bottles of booze. Once over the border, they drove into the outskirts of Lifford, where Brendan said he needed to buy some cigarettes. Pat pulled into a garage and filled up while Brendan went inside to buy his cigarettes. As he did so, he received a package from behind the counter, which he slipped inside his jacket.

They then resumed their journey, leaving Lifford and driving along a series of small country lanes. The mood in the car changed. Brendan had stopped drinking and singing while Pat drove, saying nothing. Suddenly, Ciaran knew what was happening. There was going to be no party with Jerry and his wife. Why should he be surprised? Had he not sent others suspected of giving information to the Brits for a trip over the border, never to return? Jerry could no longer trust him. The leak about the explosives in Strabane, the bomb warning in London, and the end of Munro were all too much to explain. He knew it would be useless to protest his innocence, and he knew he could not overcome someone as powerful as Brendan. When it happened, it was quick. Brendan said something about stretching our legs and nudged Ciaran out of the car, while Pat said nothing in the front. Brendan made Ciaran kneel on the side of the road, and the last thing he knew was the feel of cold metal on the back of his neck.

Jerry had given clear instructions to Brendan and Pat about what to do after they had killed Ciaran. They were to split up, with Brendan responsible for hiding the body with the help of local volunteers, who would then provide him with a car to cross back into Northern Ireland via Dundalk. On the other hand, Pat's orders were simply to retrace his steps and head back to Northern Ireland via Lifford and the Hump VCP before lying low in Strabane until required.

Pat was glad to be alone for a while and have a think. Just short of the border, he pulled to the side of the road and rested his tired muscles. His leg still ached from taking a 7.62mm round that night in Belfast a year before. Even on a warm day, it hurt, and when it rained, which it did most of the time in Northern Ireland, it was agony. Pat lit a cigarette. He had nearly lost his life that night. Since then, he had come to realise that he just wanted to survive the armed struggle against the Brits. Brendan was different. A die-hard IRA man to his core, he would do anything to drive the Brits out of his country, even if he lost his life in the process. Mary was different again, clever, pretty and passionate, but not for the IRA. She wanted a united Ireland, but not through violence. She had always wanted to escape from Northern Ireland, and, with her brains and her looks, she could do this. Pat hoped she had managed to escape, though to where exactly he didn't know.

Then there was his position. Mary had told him more than once that, if he continued to follow blindly in Brendan's footsteps, it would only be a matter of time before he took another bullet in a British ambush. So when Major Smith, or whatever his real name was, offered him a deal that day at RUC Springfield Road, he decided to accept. In return for information, Major Smith promised that there would be no SAS ambush waiting for Pat. He was also offered a small amount of money for his services. Pat knew there was no way of turning back now. The information about the explosives going to Strabane was invaluable to the Brits, and if the IRA ever discovered this, he would end up like Ciaran, or worse.

Pat climbed back in the car, started the engine, and headed to the Hump. As he passed the Brit checkpoint, he placed a road map of Northern Ireland on his dashboard, his signal to Major Smith. "All is OK for now."

Chapter Thirty-Five

The ferry made its unhurried approach to the docks on the northern edge of Hamburg, where a light drizzle and spray from the sea combined to make the passenger decks wet and slippery. Passengers were asked to return to their cars first in German and then in English. It had been a few years since he had heard German spoken; his summer holidays in Bavaria seemed an age ago.

Colin went down to his car and felt a thrill at the sight of his BMW 320i, which Johnny had looked after while he was away. It would be good to give it a good run on the autobahn south to Fallingbostel. Once settled into his car, he waited briefly for the cars in front to drive off the ferry, and he was on his way. Before he knew it, he was on the autobahn, heading south at over 100 mph in the fast lane. On both sides of the autobahn, the country was flat farmland, broken up by occasional pine forests that looked dark and damp in the rain. He had never served in West Germany before, and he guessed he would be spending a lot of time harbouring in pine forests while on exercise in preparation for a Russian invasion.

In no time, Colin saw the turning for Fallingbostel from the autobahn. Reluctantly, he slowed down, changed gear, and took the main road into town. It was Friday afternoon, and he saw some locals heading for a Gasthaus, presumably to celebrate the end of the working week and the start of the weekend. It all looked unremarkable and rather small, more of a village than a town, if not for the two British armoured brigades based nearby. Colin drove over a roundabout with a Royal Military Police Guardroom set back from the road. *Let's hope I have nothing more to do with them!* Colin thought.

Once past the roundabout, he soon saw the entrance to Wessex Barracks, his new posting. On reaching the barrack gate, he was delighted to see that Sergeant Appleby was on duty and that Corporal Pierce, who must have won back his two chevrons, was also on guard.

"Hello, sir!" said Sergeant Appleby, saluting smartly. "Been on a course, sir? Or was it a long holiday?" He was grinning cheerfully, and Colin didn't know if he was being serious or not.

"Just some adventure training, Sergeant Appleby."

He was given directions to the Officers' Mess and Colin pulled up outside a long, single-storey building. There was music playing inside.

Of course, thought Colin, *The Officers' Mess Dance Weekend.* The Regimental Adjutant had reminded him that he would be joining the same weekend when officers could invite their girlfriends from the UK to spend the weekend in Germany. Colin got out of his car and walked through what he thought was the main entrance, nearly colliding with a young girl.

"Good God, Sarah!" said Colin, astonished to be face-to-face with his sister. "What are you doing here?"

Sarah said nothing but wrapped her arms around her brother and kissed him warmly. She started to cry. Johnny Keynsham then appeared.

"Well," said Sarah, starting to explain how she was on an army base in West Germany. "Johnny asked me out for the Regimental Dance."

"Um, we have seen quite a bit of each other, actually, in London, before we came out here." Johnny looked a bit sheepish. He was saved by the arrival of his twin sisters, also clearly invited to the party, who threw their arms around Colin, giggling loudly. Colin felt bemused. Were Johnny and Sarah an item? Clearly, a lot had happened while he had been away.

Colin woke up early the next morning. He had enjoyed the previous evening, but he was not ready yet for all-night partying. He was the first to arrive in the dining room for breakfast. An officer dressed only in underpants and a bearskin cap was asleep on a sofa in the anteroom. The mess staff had tidied and cleaned up around him, taking care not to wake him. It must have been a good party. Colin tucked into his solitary breakfast of coffee, toast, and marmalade. The mess was quiet after last night's revelry. All the girls who had been invited out to stay for the weekend were put up by married officers and their wives in their quarters nearby. Sarah had told him that she and Johnny's twin sisters were staying in the Commanding

Officers' residence across the croquet lawn from where Colin was sitting.

Colin was anxious to report to the Commanding Officer. On arriving at a new unit, he knew he should report to the Commanding Officer as soon as possible. But he was not at the party last night nor in the Orderly Room yesterday afternoon. The Orderly Room Sergeant didn't appear to know where he was, which was odd. He decided to walk over to the Orderly Room and try again. He was just leaving the dining room when the Officers' Mess Colour Sergeant approached.

"Excuse me, sir," he said. "The Commanding Officer would like to see you now."

"Of course," Colin replied. "I'm just going over to the Orderly Room now."

"No, sir. He asked if you could see him at his residence. In civvies."

The Commanding Officer's house was a large building that might have been a hunting lodge if it were not inside a barracks. When Colin arrived, Jeremy was waiting for him in the hall.

"Come in, Colin," Jeremy said warmly. "It's very good to see you." Jeremy led the way into a small study on one side of the hall. Voices were coming from the terrace outside.

"Sarah and Johnny's twin sisters are doing their yoga," Jeremy explained. Colin doubted whether Jeremy knew one end of a yoga mat from another.

"Take a seat, Colin." Jeremy continued. "Sorry, I wasn't around yesterday. I had to go to…"

The door opened and in walked Jeremy's mother, Susan Kershaw, whom Colin had met at St James' Palace.

"Hello, Colin. Has Jeremy offered you some coffee?" Susan asked.

Jeremy looked a bit flustered. "Oh, really, Jeremy!"

"I'd love a coffee," said Colin.

When Jeremy and Colin were alone again, Jeremy continued.

"As I was saying, I had to go to HQ BAOR in Rheindahlen at short notice. Summoned by the general, not the Corps Commander, mind, but the Commander in Chief himself."

"What did he want to see you about, sir?"

"You, Colin."

"Me Sir?"

"Yes, you. You see, the general received a visitor from the UK yesterday; he flew over especially. Some chap called Major Smith. "Do you know him?"

Colin nodded.

"Well, of course, he's not a major. Not even in the Army. But in rank, he's the equivalent of a three-star, at least. Anyway, Major Smith says the IRA has a special warrant out for you to be killed. This is all a secret, of course. So we have to keep an eye on you. No going back to the UK for the time being, and certainly not Northern Ireland," Jeremy paused. "Or the South, of course."

Colin realised he was being told not to start looking for Mary.

"So I'm the lucky one to have you in my battalion," Jeremy said. Colin was pleasantly surprised to see that Jeremy meant what he was saying.

The door opened, and Jeremy's mother was holding a tray of coffee and biscuits. "Don't keep Colin long, dear; he hasn't seen his sister for ages."

When Colin and Jeremy were alone again, Colin spoke.

"It's great to be back in the battalion, sir, and thank you for helping me with the military police that day in Chelsea."

"Not at all. Two more things. Firstly, you've been awarded the Queen's Gallantry Medal. Of course, you won't be able to tell anyone how you earned it but many congratulations. Secondly, I'm promoting you to captain. You'll be the youngest captain in the battalion. That won't cause you any trouble, will it?"

"No, sir. No trouble."